2084

The Reawakening

Chip Kussmaul

Other books by Chip Kussmaul:

Elysian Place a Family Renovation

Trilogy- Passages From Life Stories in
the Time of Slavery

Coming soon: Breakfast at Buddy's

Copyright © 2024 by Chip Kussmaul

All rights reserved. No part of this book may be reproduced in any manner whatsoever without written permission except in the case of brief quotations embodied in critical articles and reviews.

Cover art by Carol Strebel

Title layout by Bekah Dagenbach

Inquiries can be directed to IndividualistsUnite@gmail.com

Dedicated to all who have gone before, who have faced their doubts and who have not complied.

"Stone Walls do not a Prison make,
Nor Iron bars a Cage
Minds innocent and quiet take
That for an Hermitage.
If I have freedom in my Love,
And in my soul am free,

Angels alone that soar above,
Enjoy such Liberty."
   Richard Lovelace (To Althea, From Prison)—1642

"The best way to keep a prisoner from escaping is to make sure he never knows he's in prison."

Fyodor Dostoyevsky. Ca 1860

"I know why the caged bird sings."

Paul Laurence Dunbar (Sympathy)-1899

"We are all just prisoners here, of our own device."

The Eagles (Hotel California)--1977

"I understand better now than when I first read that poem. 'Stone walls do not a prison make.' The real prison is in our mind. We can escape. No matter how physically constrained we are, we can escape the ultimate prison, our own minds."

Anonymous --2084

Since the beginnings of civilization, we have pondered what it is to be free, measured against what it is to be secure within the confines of ordered society. Some eagerly accept that order, that security, regardless of the cost in freedom.

But some question. Some doubt the sincerity of their leaders. Some feel stifled by conformity. Some contemplate reaching beyond the defined borders of their minds, and step, perhaps hesitatingly at first, into the unknown. This story, a diary, is of one such person.

Chip Kussmaul

2084

Entry One

I'm writing this, not because I want to, but because I have to. I don't know who, if anyone, will read it. If they read it, I don't know what difference it will make. Still, I have to write this.

I think I need to explain the concept, as I use it here, of "have to". No, the Central Planning Committee does not require this. Far from it. It may seem foreign to you, whoever reads this, that a person can feel an inner sense of "have to," totally apart from the teachings of our great Thought Leaders.

I was fifteen when I first had some inkling in my own mind of things that I had not been taught, but which seemed real to me anyway. I was sure that it was the Misinformation Mindset that we have all been warned about. I was going to go to my Counselor Nanny to get it straightened out, but something kept me from doing that. It's hard to say what. It's almost as if some inner ray of light, some essential reality is trying to make its way into my mind.

I was afraid, at first. Have there not been countless people who have succumbed to Indy Think, who have ultimately disgraced themselves, their families, and their Communes by expressing and acting on Disinformational thoughts? We have been taught that such people are properly reviled, and I certainly didn't want to be one of them. I, probably like you, was sure that I could never be like them. Such people are known to be lacking in essential intelligence genes, and while they are to be pitied, they must also be contained and controlled, for the sake of all of us.

I think back to those years, in school. It seems almost like another lifetime, but really not so long ago. We are all taught in school about working for the common good. And I believe that; believed it then, believe it now. But what is the common good? The Thought Leaders explain it all in the Manifesto, which they revise to keep up with the latest developments.

It makes so much sense. Everything is carefully considered and planned so that We the People can act in unison to achieve the greatest good. And I am part of this, or was, or still am.

Here's what bothers me. I feel that something is wrong, but I don't know exactly what it is or what I should do about it.

I am writing this to help me sort out my mind. But I also think that someone might read this someday in the future, and get some sense of who I am, who we are here, just as I have from this tattered old diary lying here on my desk. This old diary. I got it in the District, at a shop that I visit now and again. The things I find there seem to tell

7

me something, they communicate a time when things were different. The past matters. Many years from now, we will be somebody's past. Shouldn't we matter to them? Shouldn't those who have lived before us matter to us?

But who will read this, given that what I say here is a Violation, and I cannot let this be seen? I type into my old laptop, a relic from another day, disconnected from the line, safe, I hope, from the Crawlers. If I am caught writing this, I'll be sent to Reeducation.

I guess Reeducation is not the worst thing that could happen. But I have to wonder why I can't have my own thoughts, and express them, without having to do it on this old laptop, in secret. Something is wrong here. Is it just me? Are others thinking the same? Am I alone?

That's an odd thought to be having; Alone. No, not alone physically, alone in my thoughts. Here I am, late at night; Riley, my bestie, is sound asleep. But I can't even express my thoughts with Riley. Shouldn't I be able to? We can talk about work, we can talk about the news as it is presented to us, we can talk about applying to have a child, but I can't talk to Riley about this. I don't feel like I fit, and who do I talk to?

Yes, I know, talk to my Counselor Nanny. But I already know what she'll do. She'll tell me that Indy Think such as this happens from time to time, but that it's only a problem if you let it fester. She'll warn me about the Misinformation Mindset, just as they've always warned us about it in school. She'll guide me back into alignment with Proper Thought.

But I don't want to align with Proper Thought. I want to examine my own thoughts. Am I really the only one like this? Are there others? I want to find a way to get this out there, reveal my thoughts, and see if there are others like me. But how? Riley would leave me, at the least, or even report me, if I tried to express disagreement with the Thought Leaders.

Maybe I should leave Riley. But what does that change? If it was just between Riley and me, leaving would be an obvious thing to do. But that's not really the problem. The problem is that I am alone anywhere I go. It's not that I don't have friends and workmates. It's that I am alone in my thoughts. All others think in strict accordance with the Manifesto. I do not. I pretend to, but I don't. Are any of the others pretending?

Chip Kussmaul

Entry Two

The irony is, I work in the Ministry of Information. I used to work as an assessor there, gathering information, categorizing it, sending it on to the Compilation Department, which further assesses and categorizes and then sends it on to the Central Planning Committee. The Central Planning Committee further collates all the input and sends it on to the Thought Leaders for final assessment and Thought Pronouncements. I can't say that it isn't an efficient process, and much better than how it used to be. More efficient and better. But, better at *what*?

Is it fate that I work at the ministry of Information? Probably not. Still, my constant curiosity of the past and how it predicts the present drew me to the ministry. And once there I tried to make my curiosity dovetail with The System's procedures. I could not do it. Our present is a mirage. It is based on no reality but the artificial reality embedded in our minds by the Thought Leaders.

In a nutshell, I don't trust the Thought Leaders. I keep track. I remember things, even write them down by hand in cursive so that what I've written can't be altered by the Crawlers. People don't know, don't suspect, but Crawlers don't just search for subversive posts, they alter existing posts. They can alter a text from your mother, if they want to. And they do want to, if it serves their purpose. They can put you into a picture from a year ago, or take you out.

So, what is real? Certainly not the posts. Not the pictures. And not the streaming news. How do we even know who is alive, or if they ever existed, except if we see them live and in person? I started thinking about this a while back. Almost every picture we have is in a digital file. Everything that we read, likewise. We write things, and can modify them at will. Sure, and why not? But the Crawlers have access to everyone's files, and they can modify them, too!

What really got me going is, I took a picture of friends in front of Founder Johnson's statue about two years ago. But then Founder Johnson was disgraced, as we all know, and they removed the statue. I checked the photo in my phone, and the statue was gone from the photo! Sure, most of our posts and pics are untouched, but they are all examined. Anything that the Crawlers need changed, they change it. There is nothing that the Crawlers don't see, read and hear. If it has been digitized, the Crawlers have a copy. And what hasn't been digitized? Our very sense of reality has been digitized.

I guess reality is whatever it is that you are used to. If the past keeps changing, right before your eyes, well then, that's normal, that's reality. Why do you think the motto of the Thought Leaders is, "The only thing constant is change"? We are led to believe that it means that everything will keep improving, thanks to the efforts of the Thought Leaders and The System. But that's not what it really says. They never say they will improve anything, only that they will change it. And they do. Constantly.

Everything needs to be the latest, up to date. But I don't see anything getting better. I kind of think it's getting worse. Some of my favorite things are old things. It drives Riley crazy, but I like to collect old things from years ago. Somehow, I relate to them. I spend quite a bit of my spare time in the District. It's like another world, a world set in the past, that never found the future. I buy things from time to time, but even when I buy nothing, there is a comfort in wandering among the old things. There is constancy. There is depth. There is meaning. The items inform me about how people lived, and that informs me about who they were, what they cared about.

Chip Kussmaul

There's this old clock that I keep right here on my desk. It's so old it
has a pendulum, no electricity. It works, but only for a while, maybe
half an hour. Useless for telling me what time it is, but it's a
connection to the past, and I like that. I took the back off it once,
partly out of curiosity at how it worked, and partly in hope of making
it work properly. I studied the insides, the gears all intermeshing. It
was so complex, beyond my understanding, that I would likely do
more harm than good, so I reattached the back, and satisfy myself that
it runs for half an hour at a time. It intrigues me that there were people
who could look at the back of the clock just as I have done, and
understand how it worked, what each of the gears did. And make it
work properly.

I like to watch the pendulum go back and forth, making a rhythmic
clicking sound. It almost seems like it's trying to tell me something,
that if I get my mind in sync with the rhythm of that pendulum, things
will be revealed to me. No, not really. But it seems that way. It helps
me think.

I buy old books in the District. And I bought this diary that's sitting
here on my desk, that inspired me to start writing this journal. We're
not supposed to have them, the books, but the Thought Police, and
people in general, presume them to be so dated and useless that
enforcement against them is generally lax.

Riley complains. Why would anyone want some old diary from
someone who lived years ago? Well, I do. I am developing a sense
that these people have much to teach me. They reach out to me, in a
way.

The diary is by some person named James Butler. I know, because
he wrote his name in it. Having found this diary, I've kept my eye out

for other things, old letters and such. I initially bought them to help me learn cursive, but these old letters each have their own story to tell. One is about war. It is a woman writing, and she is telling how sad she is that her son was killed in the war. I can't imagine people killing each other, killing each other deliberately.

Yet, I also read of love and compassion. They could express love so much better than we do today. Did they only *express* the love better, or did they truly love better? I'm still not sure.

These letters let me see into the lives of people who lived many decades, even centuries, ago. They had interesting lives. Meaningful lives. More meaningful, I sometimes think, than my own.

I've found that each person's cursive varies, some by quite a bit. To learn to read cursive you have to learn the styles, how they vary, and what they have in common. I'm getting there.

What good does this do me? I don't know. Maybe it just distracts me from the present, a present that frustrates me, even worries me. It's like I'm from the past, belong to the past. I don't belong here.

And I shouldn't be writing this. It's subversive.

The books I have, that I read after Riley is asleep, are full of interesting ideas. What's surprising is that they don't all agree with each other. That's why they removed books from the library, and we're supposed to only read officially sanctioned writing. They taught us in school that there was mass confusion in the past, misinformation and disinformation, that people argued and even fought over the confusing ideas. That's why they had wars.

I can see, when I read my books, that that is true, that they have conflicting ideas. One book says one thing, but then another book says the opposite. What am I supposed to think? But here's where it gets interesting. I don't mind the thinking. My *own* thinking. I felt uncomfortable, at first, with the confusion of all these different ideas. I wanted to go back to the official Thought Pronouncements and just not stress. But after I've experienced the vast range of ideas and imagination in the old books, the Thought Pronouncements seem so simplistic, artificial.

I can't leave these books alone. I'm finding, not all questions have answers. And some questions have multiple answers. Many of the answers lead to other questions. It goes on and on! I like that! Does that make me strange? That I don't just accept the Thought Pronouncements? That I sometimes *disagree* with the Thought Pronouncements? Sometimes I catch myself thinking, 'why didn't they modify these books so that they all agree?' I have to remind myself; they can't modify them, they're *printed*, they're like this forever. Isn't that desirable?

And that's why I type this on my old antique laptop. It's so old that I have the option of disconnecting the Wi-Fi, and I have. The Crawlers can't find me here. In writing these words, I am subject to Reeducation, if I am caught.

Is that so bad? Reeducation seems to work. People get caught, sometimes, saying things or expressing thoughts that go outside the Thought Pronouncements. They get Reeducated, and everything is supposed to be fine after that. And maybe it is. Maybe the Reeducated people feel all better, readjusted and reintegrated into society. But I don't want to be readjusted. I don't want to get my thoughts aligned.

It's taken me a long time to get to this point. You can't just decide to reject the very basis of everything you've been taught. I've had to, well, *think*! Looking back, I see that there's always been a seed in my mind. A seed lying dormant, waiting for the right conditions in order to grow. It started when the Ministry transferred me to Investigations. Working as an Investigator kind of gave me a new perspective. While

I previously had assessed information, filtered for disinformation and misinformation, now I was investigating people.

Naturally, I wasn't initially thrown into anything serious, I just investigated claims against people who might have said something unflattering of the Thought Leaders, or some such. The easiest thing for such a suspect to do is just admit what they've done and take their Reeducation. It doesn't cost them much. That's generally the way it goes. Sometimes a person tries to fight it, but it never goes well. And with fighting it, they end up getting Class II Reeducation, and that can ruin a career.

So, that was pretty much what I did for over a year, investigate violations. Then I was made a Prosecutor. There's not much prosecuting involved in being a Prosecutor, since the Investigator has already made the determination. As Prosecutor, I work out a plea agreement with the defendant, and then send my recommendation to the Court which, most times, follows my recommendation. It all works pretty efficiently, and for the best. And that's the way it's been for as long as anyone remembers.

But then I had this case. And that's when that seed in my mind found its chance to grow. The case was about a guy who had put flowerpots out in front of his Dwell-Pod without a permit. And then security video showed him watering beyond the limit.

That's two infractions in one. But it still wasn't all that serious. The guy got brought into me, and I expected to resolve the issue quick enough. But he wouldn't take a plea deal! I patiently explained that he could get off with Class I Reeducation and get it all behind him without too much trouble. But he said no! I told him if he didn't take the plea, that would automatically raise the charges to Class II, and that's serious. Why not take the deal?

Chip Kussmaul

He told me, and it's been close to a year now, but I still remember, "I don't need anybody's permission to plant flowers in a flowerpot and water them."

I looked at him like he had two heads! If the Thought Pronouncements say you need a permit, then you need a permit. I told him that, and he just shook his head. "I am a free man. You can do what you want to me, but I will not give up my freedom just because you demand permits!"

I had never encountered anything like this. I couldn't decide what to do. This whole thing was about flowerpots and water. He needed a permit, which is not that hard to get, and then everything would be all right. I wouldn't normally do this, but I didn't want to go hard on this old man, so I told him that if he got the permit, I'd just drop the whole thing. He said no!

"I've watched this all develop, my whole life," he said. "It gets worse and worse. One thing after another. Now you can't live a basic life and express a basic thought without getting permission. I'm done. I'm not doing it. Do what you have to do, but I won't be getting a permit, I won't be pleading guilty, I won't be going to any damned Reeducation, and the Thought Police can just stick it. I don't care!"

I wanted to further explain the ramifications of what he was saying. The trouble is, what he said made sense! They're just flowers. Just a little bit of water. I wanted to think of something to say that was convincing to both of us, and I could come up with nothing.

It was my job to see this prosecution through, yet I could see no reason for it. I wanted to tell him I was sorry for his trouble, and just turn him lose. But that's not how it works. If the man completely refused to cooperate, that means nothing less than Cancellation. Cancellation for some flowerpots! I had never had a case that went to Cancellation. That was usually only for seditionists and conspirators and that sort, and the higher-ups handled those cases. Flowerpots?

I very nearly pleaded with the man to take my offer, but he wouldn't.

"All my life, I've tried to keep apart from this foolishness that you people do, but there is just no escaping it anymore. I'm done trying. Do what you have to do. You can do what you want to me physically, but I will not participate in your stupid Reeducation. My mind will always be my own, and you can't control it!"

I was very nearly panicked. My first thought was that people like this need to be made an example of. Otherwise, things get quickly out of control, as they have taught us about in history class. That's what my head said. That's what my education has taught me. But my heart wasn't in it.

I had a deputy take the old man to a holding cell, and went to my supervisor, I'll call her Lorna, and filled her in on the whole thing. Surely there were precedents, procedures. Something.

"Cancellation," Lorna said. "He's left you no choice. We can be very compassionate here, but we must maintain standards. And we must have compliance. If he won't capitulate, then it is, in essence, sedition. We can't see it any other way. We can't let anyone else see it any other way. You've done more than enough, bent over backwards. It's on him. He has sealed his own fate."

It was getting later in the afternoon, and I decided to just leave the old man in the holding cell overnight. I couldn't bear to bring him back into the office and charge him with Sedition II, with the recommendation of Cancellation.

I went home. My bestie had just gotten back from work, also at the Ministry, but in the Office of Equity. I casually mentioned my case. I had to be careful. Even with my bestie I couldn't express misgivings about The System. So, conversationally, I told Riley about the old man who would take Cancellation over just getting the permit.

"That's how some of those old men are, you know," Riley said. "They just can't adjust to the way things are now."

"But cancellation is so excessive. The man is harmless. Wouldn't hurt anyone. Means no one any ill will."

Riley looked at me, a bit perplexed. "It was his choice, and he's made it. I'm sick of these people who keep complaining about things, when everybody has such a good life. There's a reason we have these Pronouncements. They have been carefully considered and vetted. You should know, that used to be your job!"

Yes, it had been. And it had made sense. It still makes sense, sort of. "But he's just an old man. He has this idea of personal rights. That he doesn't need permission for every little thing. That he doesn't need to conform in everything. That he can have his own way of life. Is that so bad?"

Riley's perplexed look shifted to one of vague suspicion. "Are you siding with him? Do you know your job; your responsibility?"

I had to ease the conversation back down. It would get me nowhere. And so, here I am, back at my laptop in the middle of the night.

Entry Three

It's been a while since my last entry. I had no choice but to charge the old man, with a recommendation of Cancellation. I tried to express my condolences to him, but I couldn't be direct. People would suspect that I am sympathetic to him, which would be contrary to The System. But I got my point across to him. And the odd thing is, he seemed entirely at peace. People are anxious about mere Reeducation, yet the old man seemed entirely at peace with going to Cancellation! He was headed to the courtroom for whatever would follow. In Cancellation cases, the Cancellation Court is entirely closed. Even the prosecutor is prohibited. The evidence and the reports are in the court's hands, they don't need us to press the case.

In spite of knowing better, I shook the old man's hand and wished him well as he was led out of my office.

He smiled. "I've never been more at peace with myself. They have my body, but my mind is my own."

That old man stays with me in my memory. I try to reconcile his views with the views I know I'm supposed to hold. They clash. They clash, and I can't convince myself that he is wrong and that The System is right. I can't seem to find the answer in the present, so I look to the past. I've been spending more and more time with these old books. With no library, I just find what books I can, wherever I can, mostly in the District. It's hard to pursue any particular subject, given that I find the books randomly. But I am learning more about our past. I read a passage a month or two ago that said something like "Stone walls and iron bars don't make a prison." That seemed odd to me, but now, with the old man, I think I understand. What would I do to preserve the freedom of my mind? Preserve? Do I even *have* freedom of my mind? My beliefs, are they mine? Where do they come from? My beliefs are nearly identical to everyone else's. Are they truth? Or are they merely the collective result of the process of The System?

Something happens, when you begin to question. You pay more attention. You notice things. You consider contrary possibilities that would never have occurred to you otherwise. As I went around the usual business at the Ministry, I became aware of subtle differences in the behavior of some of my Compatriots. A person who was not watching for them would not notice them, but they are there, if you are aware.

There was one person in particular who got my attention, and I got theirs. I'll call him Ted. It was offhand talk at first. Little jokes that could be taken as meaningless if overheard, but meaningful to ourselves.

It was evident that Ted wanted to talk seriously to me as much as I wanted to talk to him, but it's not so easy to do. So, we did nothing for a long time. I think it was nearly a year. But over time, with innocuous comments, we have communicated a lot to each other without anyone suspecting. At least we hope so.

We both doubt that The System works as flawlessly as they claim. We have thoughts that contradict the official Thoughts, and feel that our thoughts are better, more genuine, than the official ones. We have been able to communicate this right under the noses of the people around us. It takes only a little nuance to say things between the lines, that others do not hear.

But it all seems so stupid. We are all worried about how we might appear to others. We all clamor to conform, not stand out. To stand out is to raise suspicion. To raise suspicion never goes well.

I've had a thought about liberty. I realize now that liberty is not the same as freedom. Liberty is something that governments give and take away. Freedom is in the mind. It is in the heart. It cannot be taken from us by governments, if we will not give it up.

The old man and his unlicensed flowerpots brought this all into focus. If I am found out, if The System finds me expressing my own thoughts, even here on this laptop in private, I could lose my liberty. But I am finally free now, and always will be, regardless. You don't know how it feels, until you have experienced it! No Influencer has the power to displace my thoughts and imagination with their own. The Central Planning Committee controls my body, but not my mind.

It took some looking, but I found that poem I had been thinking of, about stone walls not making a prison. It's by a man named Richard Lovelace, who lived centuries ago. The last stanza says:

Stone walls do not a prison make,

Nor iron bars a cage;

Minds innocent and quiet take

That for a hermitage.

If I have freedom in my love,

And in my soul am free,

Angels alone, that soar above,

Enjoy such liberty.

The strange thing is that, from what I can tell about Richard Lovelace, I disagree with him about much of what he thought. But the poem still speaks to me, in my situation, centuries later. Richard Lovelace and I are different, and separated by centuries, yet we have this poem in common.

When you have lived a certain way, when everyone you know has done the same, when your leaders watch over you and incessantly impress upon you a certain way of thinking, you are bound to come to believe that it is the *only* way of thinking. It's comfortable believing that, but I'm seeing that it's not true. I'd rather know uncomfortable truth.

We are all scared. We are afraid of anything that disrupts our uncontested sense of tranquility. I think I get it, now. That is why we are all afraid to hear a contrary opinion, a questioning of Official Thoughts. We can't handle it. We can't handle the confusion. We would have to make choices, endlessly sorting out conflicting ideas. I am coming to cherish that. But others fear that freedom. They enclose themselves in the comfort and security of accepted beliefs. They are so afraid of, and feel so threatened by unique thoughts, that they will arrest and prosecute people for having them.

I think, even, that people fear their own selves, their own tendency to question. For Riley to accept even the slightest questioning of The System, from me or from anyone, would make them feel weak, penetrable.

I see now, tolerance of other ideas is strength, not weakness. Riley cannot tolerate other ideas, because their own are so weak.

I understand better now than when I first read that poem. 'Stone walls do not a prison make.' The real prison is in our mind. We can escape. No matter how physically constrained we are, we can escape the ultimate prison, our own minds.

Chip Kussmaul

Entry Four

Now there are three of us! That third person, I'll call Mary, got the hang of our communication. They could be spying, but I don't think so. I keep a healthy suspicion to look for signs of phony support, but I see nothing but genuineness. A person can fake just about anything, but it's difficult to fake genuineness. My time as an Investigator, and now a Prosecutor, has taught me to be discerning in that regard. Having said this, I realize how many other Prosecutors just do their job. Convictions, compliance, are their goals. They don't care how genuine, how inwardly honest anyone is. There is no genuineness in themselves.

This conspiracy of three makes me much more aware. The Thought Leaders make everything about words. But the meaning of those words is often ill-defined, and there is no nuance. Shades of meaning are lost to them

I can say the correct words, but communicate something quite different from what the words say. I've found that, with just a little nuance, I can say, "The Thought Leaders did exceptionally well this time," and my compatriots know I am saying they screwed up. It also helps that those around us would never even consider the possibility of the Thought Leaders screwing up, or of anyone suggesting such a thing. So, a statement dripping with sarcasm gets right past them.

Still, what now? In my heart, I know I can't let it stay like this. As I get older, I want to know more, comprehend more, meet people with different ideas. Discuss them openly.

I have thoughts now, that I should do something to make this possible. But what? It invigorates me to not just go along, yet I can't speak out. We can't speak out.

Frankly, I'm angry. Perhaps it's not for me to decide, but I am deciding. We must change this; change the way it's been for so long. I don't want the violence, even wars, that there were when people could disagree. But I can't accept the way it is.

The Thought Police presume that there aren't enough people like us to form a large group of conspirators, nor that such a group could keep the secret among themselves. So, they primarily only watch out for two or three people meeting privately, saying inappropriate things, and nip their conspiracies in the bud.

For all I know, they're right. Right here in this one office, there's three of us. And there may be more of us, here in this office. And there are a lot of offices. If the Thought Police can find and shutdown small 'conspiracies' such as ours before they grow and connect with each other, they need never concern themselves with a full-scale movement. I want to find a way to connect with whoever else there is, without raising suspicion. It's a tough choice; accept what I have now, which isn't all that bad, or attempt much more, and possibly lose it all. Lose it all? Lose my liberty, only

I've had this crazy thought; it's been playing in my mind. What if finding conspirators, these anti-System heretics was my *job*? Crazy thought!!! But what if, in an effort to quell dissent, I was the agent for purging dissenters? That's not so very different from what I do now. After all, I am a Prosecutor.

What I do now concerns isolated incidences. But what if there were a conspiracy? Then there would have to be a concerted effort to weed them out before they could become pervasive. They used to have a Bureau of Subversion Control that did exactly that. And they had special courts specifically to arrest and convict anyone who was guilty of collusion. I didn't have to go find this information; they taught it to us in school. One of the main points of our Educational System is to teach the success of the Thought System in overcoming the radicals and extremists. It had succeeded so long ago that it is just boring history now, not a vivid reality.

But what if there was a resurgence of conspirators?! What if a need was found to reestablish inquiries into that resurgence? What if I led it? It is absurd on the face of it, but why not? If I could lead an agency assigned to find these 'heretics', I could seek them out with impunity! Clearly the downside is, how would I make allies of these people, rather than prisoners? And what good would it all do, anyway? In the end, am I chasing a foolish possibility that could yield nothing? Or, worse than nothing?

It comes down to this. I have nothing to lose. My life is not terrible. I am not suffering, at least not physically. I have the life that all the Middle Class enjoys, and you could not want more. That is, unless you want to live a life of freedom without being arrested and assigned to Reeducation.

That's a funny term, "Reeducation". Admit that having your own thoughts is a crime. Promise to never do it again, and you might get off with little punishment. I remember vaguely about something that happened many years ago, in which people were imprisoned for committing seditious conspiracy. They had done nothing physically; they had only talked about it. I used to accept their prosecution as being proper; not anymore.

No, nothing to lose. But what can I hope to gain? All these questions. All this thinking. Frankly, I find it exhilarating. If nothing at all comes of it, if I end up in Reeducation, it's all worth it. The freedom to think. I will never give that up, no matter what they do.

But wait! The old man refused Reeducation. I had no choice but to have him Cancelled. Am I prepared for that in my own case? I really don't know. There's one way to find out.

So, think I must. How can I get the Central Planning Committee to reinstate the Bureau of Subversion Control? How can I get them to put me at the head of it? How can I control the situation to the extent of finding the people I'm looking for, organizing them, and achieving something useful, without being found out for what I am?

Every bit of that is absurd! But it excites me in a way that I have never been excited. What if I could talk almost directly, in public, to the people I was seeking, but not be found out? *Very* absurd!

But advertisers do much the same. They sell products based not so much on the merits of the product, but on how a person perceives themself in using that product. That's how they sell cars. They don't advertise the car's features, they promote how good you'll feel about yourself if you buy one.

I remember an advertising expression that I found in an old book, "Don't sell the steak, sell the sizzle." What if I could sell the sizzle to the Central Planning Committee, while diverting them from noticing the steak? Get them to concern themselves only with the perception that the System isn't in full control, and leave out facts and specifics. The Thought Leaders do essentially the same thing themselves. They get buy-in from the populace by selling them the idea of peace and happiness. But what, really, is the product? I see now, that to achieve this sense of peace and harmony, the Thought Leaders have enforced conformity, a little at a time, and erased any sense of individuality. And the people don't even realize it has happened.

I want to reverse that. I think of my Bestie. Would Riley ever be willing to question the Thought Leaders, and develop independent thoughts? I'm going to try to find out. Most of what I used to believe, the trust in The System, is now suspect. I can't keep this within me and just live with it. It's eating me up. I can't go back, but I'm not sure of the way forward. I want to have an airtight plan, but I doubt that is possible.

Still, I am developing a plan. I have come to see that The System is capricious, that it acts just for the sake of appearing significant, with little regard for effectiveness or fairness. The System exists to maintain control, not administer justice. If I could control, or at least influence, who it is that gets reported for sedition, could I not manipulate The System in ways of my own choosing? No, I can't plan this precisely, but if I can keep enough control of the situation, and if others aren't watching too critically, I think I might be able to locate more compatriots, all under the nose of The System!

I am going to test The System, make it respond to me instead of me respond to it! My compatriots and I have alluded to this idea previously but have not yet acted on it.

That will now change. I've made my two compatriots understand that they should express concern to me about a seditious person they know, and to ask what they should do about it. That is something we can address in the open. We even involved some of the others in the office, who are only too willing to weigh in on how to approach such a serious matter.

I formed an ad hoc meeting in the conference room. We had been there to discuss performance reviews, but as the meeting was beginning to break up, I mentioned, off the record, that Ted had an issue with someone in data assessment.

That caught people's attention. What did he know?

"That's the thing, "said Ted. "I can't be sure. "They've made some strange statements. Maybe they were having a bad day, but they seemed to be saying that The System wasn't adequately meeting needs, and that the Thought Leaders didn't care as much as people think they do. And once when I walked into their office unexpectedly, they were on the phone, and it seemed that they quickly changed the tone of the conversation when they saw me. I think they had been discussing something subversive."

"Well, who are we talking about?" asked Carlotta.

"I'd rather not say. They seem suspicious. I sense seditionist sentiment, but I can't know for sure. I wouldn't want to implicate an innocent person."

"Certainly not," Larry responded. "But we can't just do nothing. That's how these things get out of hand."

"Damn right," added Marchon. "Nip these things in the bud. Whoever you're talking about, we'd be doing them a favor, stopping them before it goes any farther."

Carlotta agreed. "We can't afford to let things slide. Subversion, by its nature, happens right under our noses, under the noses of those who aren't vigilant. We can't let this pass."

I had been only an observer. Ted had made an innocuous statement, yet people were already eager to find this alleged subversive and bring them to justice. I would have liked for even one person to caution about jumping to conclusions. It didn't happen.

Still, the opportunity was ripe. I offered, "Perhaps the person should be monitored more closely to see if they reveal themselves in any way."

There was immediate acceptance of the idea. But what would monitoring consist of? Who would do it?

"I'm the senior member of this group, so maybe I should see to this," I said. "I can go to Lorna to get authorization."

"That's probably best," said Karen. The others seemed satisfied also.

I had no idea what 'authorization' I would be seeking, and nobody asked. But I went to Lorna and told her of our conversation in the conference room. She wanted to know what individual we were talking about. I had had the plain good sense to not bring Ted with me. I didn't know who Ted was suspicious of, I told her. He hadn't wanted to tell anyone, but with me as the authorized investigator, he would tell me without reservation.

So, I became the authorized investigator. Lorna deputized me, a perfunctory procedure for Prosecutors, giving me police power to make arrests.

Now, all we needed was a suspect! We need someone that we can accuse of participating in a conspiracy and who people would believe was actually guilty. It needed to be someone that people didn't particularly like and wouldn't defend. I wanted to see if The System protected an innocent person from spurious accusations.

We had some good choices for a 'suspect'. But then I had an inspiration. Rather than choose a 'suspect' ourselves, let the others do it.

So, we told our office mates that while we couldn't reveal the identity of the suspect at this time, we were watching them closely, and they would be the first to know, when the time came. I suspected that, over time, the group would determine a 'suspect' on their own, even when there was no suspect. They wanted to be able to say, "I knew it!" when we made the announcement.

I wanted to discover that I was wrong, but I wasn't. There was too much insecurity, too much fragility in their psyche. The finger-pointing commenced immediately. I could see that evidence was irrelevant. The social leaders of the group, over a little time, developed a mythology concerning one person, and then 'discovered' and 'recalled' damning evidence and statements attributed to her. Some of the others bought in, having their own 'recollections' and 'damning evidence'. Others simply stayed out of the way as this developed.

Entry Five

It's been about a month since my last entry to this journal. Things have been working out well, in a sorry sort of way. We apprehended the 'suspect' after monitoring her for about a month. She insisted she had never had a disloyal thought. But of course, that's what they all say!

I felt bad at what was happening to her, but she would suffer no consequences in the end. I assured her there would be no problems if she cooperated. She was not really guilty of anything, or at least, guilt is relative. But she was not as popular as others in her department, didn't try to fit in, and when the others were prompted to find a conspirator, she was a sitting duck. No one would speak on her behalf, given that they had previously condemned her. Those who had previously refrained from speaking against her, would now refrain from speaking for her, in order to protect their own self-interest. With very little effort, I had control of the dynamics.

I don't know how I didn't anticipate this moment. Maybe it's because I wasn't sure that it would work. Would the office really turn on someone, with only a little suggestion? Yes, I now know, they would. I have to think of the many times that this has probably happened, and no one even realized it. Not the people involved, not the Investigators or Prosecutors. No one. This, in a System that is supposed to protect us all, equally!

I think of the old man. There was no reason for any of it, yet they pushed him through The System for no other reason than it's The System. Before, I tentatively questioned the System. Now, I condemn it outright. Before, I wondered if it was just me, if I was the oddball who couldn't comprehend; now I know I'm not. I don't know if there are just two like me, or many thousands, millions, but I will not make it about numbers. The System is wrong. It demands compliance of us, but has no soul, no sense of the individuality of the spirit. I have been slow and reluctant to reach this conclusion, but there it is. Call me Heretic. Call me a Disloyalist. If I am those things, I have no problem with it!

My immediate problem was with what to do with this woman who I had to arrest, but could not harm. I hoped that Reeducation would work out. It would satisfy those in the office, and after Reeducation she could put it all behind her. I went through the motions of an arraignment, but assured her from the start that I saw no problem with getting the entire situation behind us.

She was surprised when we apprehended her. She swore that she had never thought or said anything inappropriate. But we had the evidence to prove her wrong. We had numerous affidavits from coworkers attesting to her subversive nature. Reading the affidavits, the suspect was perplexed. She didn't remember the occasions in the same way as the affidavits stated. Over the course of just a few days I had her convinced that she really was guilty, even if it had been unintentional. A truly innocent person would not even inadvertently make the kind of statements that others claimed she made.

I suggested that, since she was mostly a good person, I was sure she could be Reeducated. Yes, there was a significant fine, but if she refused to comply, Reeducation II meant total confiscation of all possessions and assets. I told her that if she made a full confession, I would recommend Reeducation I. I well remember the look of relief! She would say anything I wanted. Confess to anything I asked her to, if she could get off with Reeducation I.

I never processed the fine. I am personally seeing to her Reeducation. I feel like a creep, that I have done this, but I dare not reveal myself.

Chip Kussmaul

My convictions concerning The System are valid, but I cannot honestly say that I am above reproach. I see now that nearly anyone can be accused and convicted of almost anything. It's frightening. How many has this happened to? How many *will* it happen to?

And what do I do now? I can't keep prosecuting, following the protocol, when I know how hollow it is. I can resign, but that only gets me out from under; it doesn't eliminate the problem. There are innocent people who need to be protected, and perhaps I have a unique means of protecting them. As far as I know, I and my two conspirators are the only ones in the ministry who are even aware there is a problem.

And, speaking of problems, with my recent success at uncovering a 'seditionist' within the ministry, there are now more people being accused of sedition. Call it blood lust, call it a pack mentality, call it what you want. But people are being reported who are guilty only of not speaking and not behaving in accordance with the expectations of the unofficial social 'leaders' in the office. It's ironic as all get-out. Here I am, the subversive that they all fear, and innocent people are being reported to me for subversion.

I remember reading about the Salem witch trials. This is like that. Except that I know they aren't witches. I started this, now I need to find a way to see it through without harming innocent people.

The Salem witch trials. The prosecutor was convinced that there *were* witches and that what he was doing furthered the cause of justice, protected the community. We think of that as ancient history, in a time when people weren't so wise. We are no wiser, now.

In less than two weeks, I have had two more cases brought to me. I could track both to instances of bad blood and office rivalry. One was a strategic move by one clique to gain political advantage over another clique.

I am on a tightrope. I could have called out the 'leaders' for their hypocrisy and vindictiveness, but they would have turned on me, and I have no idea how that might work out. The accusers supplied affidavits that had official bearing, but were absurd in fact. This is The System! I work the cases through and get the defendants nice, easy Reeducation I. That process has worked somewhat to the advantage of the defendants, with relocation to offices away from their accusers. I like to think I benefited them overall.

But maybe I'm just kidding myself. I started all this just to see if I could do it, just to see if my suspicions were right. I never thought about how right I might be. And now I wonder if I should have just left well enough alone. What have I done? Is it my fault that I have started this? Or their fault that it works? At the very least, we are all flawed, and The System does nothing to counter it. Exacerbates it, even.

But the third case caused more concern. Or joy, depending on how you look at it. He was a believer! In a one-on-one interview, it was easy enough to see. But what could I do? He refused to go along. He would not confess, even if there was no punishment. He could not be convinced, cajoled into believing he had done anything wrong. He challenged me on it. He *challenged* me rather than defend himself as he should! He called out The System for its hypocrisy! He would not enter Reeducation.

The old man came back to mind. Cancellation came to mind. This man, being in the Ministry, was more aware than most of the ramifications. But he, like the old man, would take Cancellation over Reeducation. I felt guilty. This might never have happened if I hadn't tried to test my hypothesis about how corrupt The System is. I begged the man to just take the Reeducation and get it over with. I told him I could make the fine go away. He would have none of it. He would not confess to impure thoughts or to subverting anything.

I guess, when you don't know what to do, do nothing. I was able to get him released on bail. I even managed to get him transferred to another department. Maybe, in time, I can drop the charges, and no one will notice. I have grown a bit, within myself, since I prosecuted the old man. I didn't strictly follow protocol in this case, and I made it work out. Things can work so much better, when you think for yourself rather than follow the rules.

But the floodgates are open! I get more and more cases. Suddenly, people believe in witches! What authorities do I turn to, when the authorities are the problem?! The good news is, I've been finding out there's more than two of us. A *lot* more than two of us!

And, bless their hearts, people are finding witches in the general population. I mean, seditionists'. I remember how alone I felt, not so long ago. Not so long ago, I was trying to find anyone who saw what I saw, thought as I thought. I'm not feeling so alone now! But I still have to keep things under wraps. If it were known what is playing in my mind, well Cancellation is not out of the question.

They say that in the witch trials, those who insisted on their own innocence were presumed to be witches because only witches would deny their sin; good people readily confess. Those who confessed were witches also, but they might be redeemable if they properly begged forgiveness of their sins.

During the height of the madness, little thought was given to the possibility that the accused might be innocent! The lives of the accused were quite literally in the hands of people who would judge the sincerity of their confessions to crimes that had never happened! Totally innocent people were hanged, because they would not admit to being witches.

The book in which I read about this says that it was really about weeding out non-conformists, individualists. People who put their self- identity and self-respect ahead of the dictates of their culture were the ones who were hanged. The witch trials were a sort-of test; those who were willing to subjugate their individuality and self-respect by confessing their sins, confessing their transgressions against the will of the people, and who begged forgiveness, generally lived. Those who refused to capitulate, were hanged. Is it really all that different today? We don't hang them these days, but otherwise the parallels are frightening!

"Make lemonade," they say, when someone finds themselves surrounded by lemons. So, I am taking advantage of my position to do workarounds for the believers any way I can. They mostly end up out on bail, but I can't keep doing this. People in the Ministry will want to know what's up, why the cases aren't settled. As for those innocent witches who have been caught up in this hunt, I find ways to get them through the process as painlessly as possible.

My conspirator, Ted, is now my deputy assistant. My supervisor readily agreed to let me appoint him. I had only to tell Lorna that there were signs of a deeper conspiracy than we had anticipated, and that I would need help. So, I had a partner in crime, so to speak. Our third conspirator, Mary, does not directly participate. She stays on the sidelines, able to innocuously sway opinions as needed. I find that it is easy to sway people whose lives revolve around being led. The trick is to lead them en mass. Work them slowly but deliberately. In the end, they will believe just about anything.

Mary had a situation that was heating up, heading toward more accusations against innocent people. She managed to turn the tide against the accusers, convincing some people to make counter accusations against them. Once the accusers saw that they stood to lose, they backed down. What is going on here? Do they not see? Do they not care?

It's funny. I knew there was a problem. I decided that I would do something about it. But I didn't know what. And I still don't know, exactly. I wanted to find a way to locate believers without tipping my hand. Now, they are being brought to me! So many of my peers, most of my peers, desire to be led. Emotionally, they seek someone who will lead them such that they need make no decisions, nor have to form their own opinions. Even our titular leaders are really followers. So, with only a little campaigning, I am now the head of the newly reformed Bureau of Subversion Control. Somehow, I made it happen, even if I didn't have it all figured out. But now I've got more to figure out. I am finding the believers that I wanted to find. But, what to *do* with them?

The believers are viscerally opposed to Reeducation, even if it is physically harmless. Reeducation would cage their sense of freedom, and they will not do it.

I have a conundrum. My plan is working almost too well. I am finding the believers. They are being delivered to my doorstep, as it were. If they will not go to Reeducation, that leaves Cancellation. But what is Cancellation? There are rumors and legends, of course, but nobody knows for sure. I need to find out.

Entry Six

How do I casually ask the Judge, "What is Cancellation?" Cancellation is so complete, that no good citizen would have any reason to want to know what it is. Honest people don't get Cancelled, and those who get Cancelled are worthy of no further consideration.

The Cancellation Courts are necessarily secretive. If a Prosecutor, as I have become, recommends Cancellation, that's pretty much it. The Cancellation Courts make a final assessment, but it's rare that a Prosecutor's recommendation is not followed. Apparently, in years before, the Courts made the findings, not the Prosecutors. And they even had open courtrooms and juries of their peers, as I've seen mentioned in old civics books.

I need a way to find out what Cancellation really is. It seems unlikely that it means death, since that goes against all the Thoughts of the Thought Leaders. But is it possible that the Thought Leaders don't have authority over the Judges? Nobody seems to know. I have been able to discern so much, but the Cancellation Court has been nearly impenetrable.

I discussed this with my compatriot, phrasing the discussion in such manner as it aroused no notice. He suggested that, instead of trying to find out what Cancellation is, we should consider what it is intended to accomplish. Knowing the why would inform the how.

That ended up being a simple conversation. Cancellation is intended to keep the Thought Process pure. Those who will not adhere strictly to the Thought Process need to be removed so as not to taint it. That is the point. People react to Cancellation with fear, but its only intent is to remove free thinkers, believers, from the population. It was never represented as punishment; still the populace is generally terrified of it. That's worked well enough for the Prosecutors. The threat of Cancellation is all it takes to get most people to agree to Reeducation. I have found that people, apart from the believers, have little dread of Reeducation. Essentially, if I say they need it, they believe they need it.

But not Cancellation! Anything but Cancellation! Yet, we can find no reason to think that Cancellation is punitive. When Ted and I considered the possibilities, it seemed that Cancellation was a place more than it was a thing. Where were these people sent to?

The most obvious way to find out was hazardous: If we could follow a Cancelled individual out of the Courthouse, we could merely follow to wherever they were taken. But we could not be known to be following. It would be Untruthful, at the very least. I know of nothing that says we can't do this, but there is no common knowledge of where the Cancelled are sent, or how they get there, so it must be a secret, even if no one said so.

We took it one step at a time. It seems almost silly, the way we did this, but we could not risk using normal electronics or GPS. When one of the Prosecutors sent a Citizen to be Cancelled, I casually followed. I couldn't risk following behind all the way, but I followed long enough to see the Citizen loaded into a carry-all van. The Citizen was placed in, but no one else got in with him. I assumed he was locked in. The van had only a small insignia indicating Thought Police, but otherwise it was entirely normal looking. It could have been delivering groceries. It drove out of sight, going west on Leadership Way.

And that was all for today. A few days later, I made it a point to unsuspiciously be walking west on Leadership Way at the point I had lost sight of the van. After a while, the van went by. I could then see that it continued west without turning, again going out of sight. My compatriot and I found ways to discuss this without saying anything unusual. We couldn't surmise any other place that it would be going, except to be going further west, so he committed to being on Leadership Way, even farther west. As long as there was no risk, we figured we could keep doing this until we found a destination.

Then, we realized that there were a number of these vans, all travelling the same route, so they were a little easier to track; lose sight of one, wait for the next one. There seemed to be no schedule, but they perhaps averaged one every hour or so.

We found, as we have in many other things, that when we just look for answers, they aren't so hard to find. The vans go to the Wall, through the West Gate, into the Wilderness.

Chip Kussmaul

Entry Seven

It's interesting how things change. I've reread all of my previous entries. It almost seems like another person wrote them. It's been less than two years, and I no longer feel emotionally isolated. Rather than feeling confined by the repressive System, I feel invigorated! It is a challenge to find ways around The System, to make the connections that need making, right under the noses of the Thought Police. Certainly, I no longer feel guilty about thinking for myself.

It occurs to me that, given that I don't know who will read this or when, I should not presume that the reader is aware of the life that I so take for granted. I have some time, as we consider what move to make next, to describe some of the specifics of our life. If it is all familiar to you, you may see no need to read all of this.

It is the year 2084. I started writing this a little over two years ago, in 2081. When I started writing this, I was more timid. I wanted to reveal nothing about myself, for my safety and yours. But I'm feeling a little bolder now. I know what I can get away with, and how to get away with it. It's never good to be over-confident, but I'll reveal what seems expedient.

I live in the northeast sector, in Coreopolis. As near as I can tell, this city used to be named Pittsburgh, Pennsylvania; or at least Coreopolis is near to where Pittsburgh, Pennsylvania used to be. When the Thought Leaders replaced states with sectors, they also changed the names of the cities, and even moved some of them. They said it was to align with the New World Order, but I have since come to think it was to erase as much history as possible. Few people today see any connection, by name or in any other way, between today's cities and those of the not very distant past. Borders are not as they were. As a result, there is little collective memory linking today with even the recent past.

And no walls! In the past they had no walls around the cities! Except for some of them. I think about how exposed the cities were to infiltration by extremists and terrorists. How could they live with that continual threat? And, sure enough, terrorists sometimes bombed people, or shot them with guns that could fire repeatedly with just one pull of the trigger. How could they have any peace of mind with that constant threat?

So, today, the Wall protects us. We have complete peace. But I wonder now, what has it cost us? No, the extremists and terrorists can't get in, but we can't get out. It's too dangerous in the Wilderness. At least that's what they say. But I now know that The System is built around self-perpetuation, not around human needs. Curiosity is banned. No, no law against being curious, but you'd best keep it to yourself. The Manifesto is looking more and more to me like a means to keep us contained, rather than the means to freedom that the Thought Leaders proclaim. And so, I wonder. Why is that Wall there? Is it to keep others out, or to keep us in?

We all are taught in Truth School that we are much better off now, and perhaps we are. But we can't really know, because we have no way to make comparisons. Coreopolis is only twenty-five years old, and information on Pittsburg is difficult to find. The only reason I know as much as I do about it is because of the old books. Real books.

I mentioned earlier, I get most of my books in the District. It's a different world, not just because of the old shops, but because the people are different. They seem to think more expansively than in the regular city. It is because of them that I started to wonder about our lives in the regular city. In the regular city things seem so structured, right down to our everyday thoughts. I began to realize that our discussions are not avenues to discovery, but are merely reaffirmations of what we've been taught to believe. I might never have noticed, but the more time I've spent in the District, the more I've seen how open they are there to the variableness of ideas. They don't feel threatened by disagreements. They just have them, and are fine with it.

Since childhood, we have been warned about the District. We are warned about the people, the bad influence. About the crime. Yes, there is crime, but that doesn't make everyone there a criminal.

Like all good citizens, I stayed away from the District. Then a friend who had a cousin that lived near the District invited me to go there. He said there were things to do that didn't exist in the regular city. I declined at first, heeding the warnings I've received my whole life, but I guess it was just my age or something, and I went with them.

I couldn't immediately assess the District, because I had no basis by which to assess it. It was an entirely new experience, but the one thing I recognized was that it was not as it had been told to me. Even with the 'used' look, it had an attractiveness. Maybe quaintness. I don't know, but I felt comfortable there. My friends wanted to do the rides at the amusement park, and I went on some with them, but I was more curious about the shops. I talked them into going into some of them. They had no problem with going into the candy store, but I also wanted to check out some of the other places. As a tag along, I was pretty much required to do what they wanted. But I went back on my own. I visited those shops. And it just went from there. I think maybe I know more about history from the District than I do from the history classes I took in school. I know of the people of the time better. History classes look at the past like it's mute and untouchable, but in the District, I roam among the history, immerse myself. The antiques. The people themselves seem from another time.

It makes me wonder why we live like we do in the regular city. Not the buildings or streets or such, but why we are so stifled. Is it what we want, or has it been forced upon us?   Both? It's a strange incongruity, the District and the regular city. The Thought Police are ever present in the regular city, but hardly at all in the District. The Thought Police have the same authority in the District that they have here, but infractions that bring severe penalties in the regular city go unenforced in the District.

I've come to see that people in the District just won't tolerate it, so it doesn't happen. I've thought about the conspiracy that Ted and I manufactured, that started this all. The witch trial, as I've come to call it, concerning the woman that with little prompting was 'discovered' to be a subversive. She even confessed, convinced that if we all said she had committed a crime, then it must be so. What if I tried to do that here in the District? What if my compatriots and I dropped a hint that there was a subversive among them who must be investigated 'before it's too late'? "Too late for what?" I hear people of the District asking, in my imagination. They don't care. Conspire to your heart's content. They don't care!

They don't care that I buy the books. After all, they're the ones selling them. They don't need to know why I buy them, and some are only too willing to discuss history, and current events, for that matter. The conversations are unguarded. No need to concern yourself with saying a wrong word, expressing a wrong thought. If they are offended at anything, they will say so, and that's the end of it. No need for Thought Police, no need for Prosecutors.

How can this exist so close to a place where people are arrested and prosecuted and coerced into supplication? I think I get it, now. Because the most secure prisons, the ones most difficult to escape, are in our minds. Freedom could be physically across the street, but some people will never get there. Apparently, they don't want to.

Why don't I live in the District? I think about it. I keep thinking about it. But getting the permit would be nearly impossible. Yes, I am free
45

in my mind, but I do not have the liberty to do as I please. I would have to resign as a Prosecutor, and even with my desire for freedom, that makes me stop and think. I would have to give up all my previous training and start over, learning new skillsets and approaches. Not easy, but it's looking more desirable all the time. I don't know, maybe someday I will try.

Thinking is tough, and some people feel threatened by the uncertainty. After all, thinking is a manifestation of uncertainty. With our Thought Leaders disseminating our thoughts to us, we need never suffer any anxiety concerning gathering information and finding truth. The Thought Leaders do all of that for us. But in these old books there are all kinds of opinions about all sorts of things, and I am left to try to sort out the truth from it for myself. Yes, it made me very uncomfortable at first, but I've come to relish the chance to immerse myself in issues. It helps me to better understand myself and my own way of thinking. Hell! It has developed my ability to think at all, something you will never learn to do from following the Thought Leaders.

Apparently, for instance, people used to argue about climate change. Some said it was caused by man while others said it was a natural occurrence. I've found a number of books about it. The strange thing is, whatever book you read, it makes some amount of sense. I've read, and I've thought, and I can't say that I see where either point of view is entirely right or wrong. It seems evident that there has always been natural climate change, but that man has had some effect on it. And, why not? What's funny is that the books tend to just take one side and argue as if the other side couldn't possibly be true. Near as I can tell, both sides are true. But what leaves me scratching my head is that some of the authors claimed that life on earth would be destroyed in the future. Yet, here we are today, living in what was their future, and we're all still here, and all doing OK. Yes, there's still the same floods and storms that there have always been. But we're better than ever at predicting them and protecting ourselves from them. I really don't get what all the fuss was about in the first place.

And what really seems strange is that these points of view seem to be related to political parties. Political parties are from the time before the New World Order and the Thought Leaders. Back then the idea was that citizens, plain citizens, would be responsible for deciding who the leaders were, and would also tell the leaders what they wanted them to do. But, near as I can tell, the political parties developed enough power that the citizens were pretty much left out. The political parties largely elected their own people, and created their own issues, rather than seek input from the citizens.

I'm not sure how I feel about this. We all have been taught that the average citizen isn't smart enough to know what's best. So, how could they reliably choose the best leader? We now have votes of affirmation rather than election. The Selection Committee selects the officials, and we affirm. No muss, no fuss. It does seem best to have the Selection Committee make those choices. Still, the more I read, and the more I think, I can see that the Selection Committee doesn't always pick the best leaders. And, anyway, who selects the Selection Committee? Now, *that's* an interesting question that I would like to have answered!

But Riley doesn't think that way, doesn't question. Riley has absolute trust in the Thought Leaders, just as they have been trained to do. Just like everyone has been trained to do. I haven't been taught differently, but somehow I've ended up seeing things differently. It makes my relationship with Riley difficult. We can't discuss this directly because they might report me, and that would really blow my cover, and all that I am doing now.

I can only make the occasional oblique reference to the idea of individual thought processing. Riley is happy with the way things are,

47

believes things that I doubt, and we can't even discuss them, sort them out. And that just makes me question still more. It seems to me that if the Thought Leaders' thoughts are so unassailably correct, then they should let us assail them. Then their Thoughts could be truly tested, and proven to be true.

Or not. And I'm beginning to think that the Thought Leaders are not so sure about their own Thoughts. That they don't want them tested, because they might not hold up.

That's what books have done to me. They've forced me to think. I don't just get information and ideas from them, they are like a catalyst, and I end up thinking my own thoughts, getting my own ideas. It's confusing, but it's also invigorating. It's like being at the top of a mountain and being able to see for long distances in all directions, while others are down in the valley, seeing only a little, and thinking it's the entire world.

Here's something that really concerns me; I'm beginning to see that our Thought Leaders themselves live in that valley. They don't see all, and so their Thoughts are not expansive, but actually quite limited. I know it sounds conceited, but I think my own thoughts are better, more informed, than theirs. I don't say that lightly, and I shouldn't say it at all. If I could explain my way out of anything else I've said before, I could not explain my way out of presuming to be a better thinker than the Thought Leaders. No, I should not have written those words, but there they are. There they will stay. I can no longer self-inhibit for the sake of comfort and security. As I write these words, it makes me wonder if I can continue on with Riley. We are too different, now. Riley has not changed. I have.

Entry Eight

I look back, now, at what has been over two years' worth of entries, and it seems sometimes like I'm reading about someone else. Yes, I know I wrote all that, but the beginnings of it seem so different than now. I started writing this as a way to sort out my thoughts. I don't think I could simply imagine my way to where I am now. Writing helps me sort things out and get them to make sense. And I think I want others to see this. It was always my intention that others would, someday. I'm nearly bursting at the seams to tell others my thoughts, to help them sort things out also, in whatever way they choose. I really believe, one day, that will be possible. And I hope to make it sooner than later.

At first, I just needed to vent, to express myself. But a vague idea has become at least a possible reality. There are many others like me. We have found ways to communicate. If you spend some time working things out, sometimes solutions can be found right in front of you. Like cursive, for instance. Even the best AI can't read cursive, these days. I suppose they could if they were programmed to, but the programmers have never bothered. The programmers can't read cursive themselves and would not know where to begin to train AI to read it. Yes, of course they could find an expert, and train AI. It's just that they don't. They can't be bothered. This airtight technological society is proving to not be so airtight, and that is encouraging.

Anyway, cursive is an excellent way for us believers to communicate among ourselves. We can't overdo it. If cursive started showing up everywhere, then the Thought Police would get suspicious. But a slip of paper mixed in with other things, here and there, arouses no suspicion. We can use new paper, as we have found ways to make it look aged. If a Thought Police sees it among other things, and we always keep our messages mixed in among other papers, they will never have reason to suspect. And there is near zero chance that a Thought Police would be able to read cursive. Or even want to.

All I'm getting at is that there are more and more of us, and we are able to communicate to a degree. But this is cause for concern. The more of us that there are, the more possibility of being discovered; the more possibility of being infiltrated. I learned a trick from one of my books. It was about the Underground Railroad. It wasn't a real railroad; it was a loose knit organization to help escaped slaves in the South of the Old USA to escape to New Canada. They don't teach this very much anymore, but it was well known in earlier times. Anyway, the people involved did not know very many other people. Escaped slaves were taken from 'stop' to 'stop' by separate individuals who only knew very few of the other stops. That way, even if one was caught, they could reveal very little information about the entire organization. So, I've tried to keep it like that in our organization. Our organization doesn't even have an exact name. That makes it more difficult to track. There are several terms that we use to refer to ourselves, and we continually shift to other terms. Even a Crawler, if it came across anything, would find little connection. And I needn't mention any of those names here.

But those slaves escaped *to* someplace. I feel that, like the slaves of two and a half centuries ago, we need a place to escape *to*. There is the District. But there is an invisible line that separates us from the district. We can cross as visitors, but it is difficult, if not impossible, to move there. If many applied to move there, it would raise flags. I know that, if it came to it, there would be another wall built, separating us from the District.

I guess there are real prisons after all, not just the ones in our minds. And we are in one. I must consider what's on the other side of that Wall. Could we live there? Is it dangerous? Would the danger be worth it? Most of all, how do we get past the Wall?

Chip Kussmaul

Entry Nine

I must do something. Our plan continues to work too well. More and more people are being brought in, accused of subversion, of conspiracy to commit sedition. I can weed out the unfortunates who simply got caught up in office intrigue. They readily confess and effortlessly submit to Reeducation. But the believers? My compatriots in freedom; what am I to do? They will not submit to Reeducation and are willing to be Cancelled. More and more of them. I've released a few on their own recognizance, but I can do only a little of that or people will complain. Worse yet, become suspicious. After all, I sold this whole Bureau of Subversion Control charade to the Central Planning Committee based on my professed desire to rid our Great Society of Disloyalists.

I can't appear soft. When it comes up, I tell my peers that we're holding some of the most dangerous offenders, hoping to crack them into turning in others. That excuse won't last forever, though. The only option, according to Law and Custom, is Cancellation for those who refuse Reeducation. I've searched my mind for another way, something that would be acceptable and not raise suspicions. I've come up with nothing. Honestly, I've doubted myself. If their system is so rigid and inefficient, then why is there no way around that system?

I've found a way to work my 'investigation' within The System, right under their noses. I've used The System to my own advantage. It's all *working*! Except for Cancellation. I must focus on that. I've cracked everything else; I can crack this.

What is really going on with Cancellation? Why can we not participate in the hearings? We are the ones sending the suspect to them, with documented charges. Why aren't we there for the trial? What is going on? Where do the vans go? We need to find out. That means we must go outside the Protected Zone, into the Wilderness outside the Wall, because that's where the vans go. And that raises a thought: The vans go out steadily, and appear entirely unarmed. How dangerous is it out there, really? They tell us to not even think about going out there because of the danger. We can fly from one city to another but, both for the sake of energy conservation and for protection from attack, we cannot drive. Besides, the car batteries won't get you from one city to another.

It used to make sense, what the Central Planning Committee and the Thought Leaders tell us. But now I doubt them. Now I question. I had a radical thought of confessing and getting myself Cancelled. I could see for myself what is out there. The thought appeals to me, but I can't do that. That would reveal our network, our Underground Railroad with no place to go. I can't confess. Someone else could, though, but who? And what good would it do?

I know we could easily send one of our believers for Cancellation. It's what we're *supposed* to be doing. If we sent one of them, who knows what we'd be asking them to sacrifice? What good would it do? Could they get word back to us? The more I've thought about it, the more incredulous I am that we know nothing about it. No leaks, not even rumors about Cancellation.

Chip Kussmaul

Entry Ten

I discussed this issue with Ted. It isn't outside the parameters that we could be expected to discuss, so we can discuss it openly. The less secretive we are, the less suspect we are. We both can find no other way to uncover Cancellation than to send a believer to Court on a charge, with a recommendation of Cancellation. We need to find the right person, discuss our plans, and get them to agree to it. It might be dangerous to them, might be dangerous to us. It might all be for nothing, but it might reap rewards. It is all we have, so we'll do what we can with it.

We went through the files of likely "suspects". We had over two hundred and, as I've mentioned previously, it makes me a little anxious that we are sitting on these cases. It doesn't look good to have too many open cases. Ted and I know all of these suspects, having interviewed them extensively. And they know us.

We've narrowed possibilities fairly quickly down to four people. We discussed them, but it was pretty evident all along that we wanted to talk with "Joe". He is older, and has lost his wife. His antagonism to The System was likely a result of his feelings of loss. His wife had held him in check, and now she was gone. He didn't care if neighbors reported him. My compatriot and I decided to have him brought to the interrogation room; to meet with him privately would have raised suspicions. The interrogation room has audio and video, so no one could accuse us of hiding anything. We were confident that "Joe" would readily perceive our intent, and that we could communicate in double-speak that would not alarm anyone watching at a later date. Following is from the official transcript of that interview. You can see that our true intent is not easily recognizable, unless you are aware of it.

Me: We are concerned about you, Joe. We do not feel that your crime rises to the level of automatic Cancellation. But if you will not accept Reeducation, it could become necessary for us to send your case to the court with a recommendation of Cancellation. Is there some reason you will not accept Reeducation? It's a simple enough process, and you can be done with it in a month.

Joe: Yes, I am aware of all that you say. But I see myself as having a right to whatever opinions and beliefs I want, and to express them whenever I wish to.

Ted: Yes, we get that. But the law is the law. You are in violation, and it is our duty to enforce the law. We're trying to help you out here, but we have our job to do.

Joe: I have no disrespect for you. Do what you have to do. And I will do what I have to do.

Me: So, we're all doing what we have to do. I guess that's that. But tell me, have you given thought to what Cancellation is, and what it could do to you?

Joe: Frankly, I have no idea. I simply will not submit to Reeducation, so the rest is up to you.

Ted: We'd like for you to consider the possibilities.

Joe: You don't know what Cancellation is either, do you?!

Me: Well, no we don't. We'd all like to, but I'm sure the Cancellation Court has its reasons for keeping it secret, and who are we to question its reasons? Certainly, my natural curiosity wants to know what it is, but I don't see a way to know. It's not like anyone who has been Cancelled has ever sent word back to tell us.

Ted: Of course, I'm sure they're not allowed to, or maybe they're not able to. Even if our Central Laws forbid execution or physical punishment for any reason, well, we can't be entirely sure of what might happen in Cancellation.

Joe. No, we can't really know. But I said, I'll take what comes. I don't hold anything against you. I have cooperated fully, and will continue to cooperate. My only regret is that I won't be able to communicate with my daughter. I won't, will I? I've always heard that Cancellation is complete. No one is heard from again.

Me: That is the case. A person would have to subvert the intention and the technology of Cancellation to communicate back to the Populace. I'm sure every technical means is employed to keep that from happening.

Joe: I'm sure you're right. I was just asking. It's not as if a person could just send a handwritten note!

Me: I don't know how a hand-written note could get back here.

Joe: Of course not. An organization that has all the latest communication and surveillance would certainly have a means to keep handwritten notes from coming in.

Ted: I think that's safe to say. You know that no one is allowed in or out of the Wilderness, except by official vehicles. The vans that take people for Cancellation are driverless, so nobody is in them on the return trip that can carry a letter or such

Joe: Well, if you knew when the van left, and when it got back, and divided by two, you might have a good idea of how far it went.

Me: That presumes that I would have any reason to want to know. And it still wouldn't tell me what direction or anything else, so it's a moot point, as far as I can see.

Joe: Hey, I'm just talking, here. I've got nothing better to do.

Ted: Yes, I get that.

Joe: If someone wanted to send a note back, they'd have to attach it somehow to the van, without anyone knowing. It might be possible, it might not. Who knows?

Me: Yes, who knows.

Joe: One thing for sure, I guess; I'm about to find out.

Me: I'm afraid that's true. You've left us with no choice. We've given you the chance, but you've made your intentions clear. So, I think we have to proceed, based on the findings of this interview.

Entry Eleven

And so Joe was remanded to the Cancellation Court for final disposition of his case. It would take a few days, and Ted and I got busy. We needed to tell one van from another and hopefully know which one took Joe out, so that we could find a way to check it for messages when it came back.

Knowing what we needed to do, we checked the lot where the vans are kept. They are not a security vehicle, so they are easy enough to get to. They are all kept in a lot next to the general service taxis. We can get to them quite easily; the trick was to not be spotted. We both considered possibilities, and then decided, once again, that being secretive would arouse suspicions. Instead, we would find a reason to be there, and hope no one thought twice about it. Any plausible excuse would do. We also needed a reason to be there more than once, since we would need to inspect the vans over time, to see if we could find any message.

I thought about how we got to this point. I had gotten myself put in charge of weeding out believers by pretending to be a dedicated Prosecutor. I really have been doing my job, weeding out believers; I'm just doing it with an entirely different motive than prosecution! So, why not use the same method to be able to freely inspect the vans? I let it be known in the office that I had been informed by a 'suspect' that the vans were being compromised by radicals, and that I thought they should be inspected regularly. Everyone thought that was a good idea, but of course no one wanted that responsibility. So, I volunteered to do it. They all thanked me.

I then went, with Ted, to the van lot. There was a small building that contained both the service bays and the small office. From here vans were assigned as needed. We went in and introduced ourselves. There were three people inside, one was clearly in charge. He sat at a desk with a placard that said 'Carl Johnson'. We presented our credentials and explained that we had reliable intel that the vans were being compromised.

"That's impossible," said Carl. "We keep track of things. Nobody comes in here that we don't know about."

"I'm sure of that," I said. "But we've been given the assignment, and we must see it through. We don't want to disrupt your operation; we'll do all we can to stay out of your way."

Carl gave what I can best describe as an aggressive shrug. He wasn't happy, but he wouldn't fight it. "Do what you've got to do, and I'll do what I've got to do. We've been here for years, no problem. Suddenly, they've got a problem. You've got to wonder what makes those people tick."

I should have let him vent, but I couldn't resist. "Those people are our superiors, having proved superior ability to manage The System. We should always trust their judgement."

His attitude changed instantly. "Well, of course. I didn't mean to suggest anything different. They know better than me, and if they need you to inspect the vans, then of course you need to inspect the vans."

That was too easy. I resented myself for playing the very game that I've been trying to undermine, but it was harmless enough, this time. Still, I want to maintain a cooperative relationship. Who knows how things might develop in the future.

"I appreciate your cooperativeness. And I assure you, I will cooperate with you. I don't want to interfere with your own responsibilities here. I'm sure we'll be able to work well together in the future."

59

Chip Kussmaul

"Of course," Carl said.

He didn't sound convinced. I would work to smooth things out later on.

Ted and I went out to the lot. The vans of course have automatic scanning monitoring for electronic bugs, so we couldn't use any sophisticated device to track them. Their GPS coordinates as they drove are tracked automatically by the DHS, but I have no connections there.

But the vans do have odometers. We could record each odometer's milage reading, and at least get some idea how far they traveled. It might tell us something. If they all were going to the same place, they would show the same milage increases, and we could determine that distance. If they went to different places, we might also be able to make some determinations in that regard. But we mostly wanted a way to communicate with Joe, assuming it would in fact be possible for him to communicate.

I had an epiphany, sort-of. I had been trying to find a way to predetermine which van Joe would be in, and a way to track it. But here we were, with free access to every van. We could check all of them for a communication from Joe, pretty nearly any time we wanted to. In finding his communication, we would know that that van was the one to check for milage. We wouldn't learn everything, but we would learn a lot. We checked the passenger compartment. I wanted to find someplace where notes could be hidden. I didn't think that the vans were all that carefully inspected between trips, but I would find out. I would casually ask Carl about their security protocol on our way out. I didn't want to get him any more riled up than I already had. I would have to work it in, in casual conversation. But I needed to know.

But, for now, Ted had found that the armrest pulled up easily enough and that there was a seam that could be pulled apart enough to hide a note. But that put another thought in my mind; would Joe be allowed to bring pen and paper with him? For now, it appeared we would have to gamble on that. Well, wait! We could put the paper into the seam on every van. Would a pen fit? We determined that some small writing device would fit, and determined to find something appropriate. So, no, Joe would not have to have anything on his person, but he would need to know what to do.

And we would have to get that paper and pen into those vans, soon. Joe might be sent away very soon, in as little as three days, which was when his hearing was scheduled. We couldn't do another inspection in that short amount of time without raising suspicion, not to mention raising Carl's ire. We decided to stop where we were, having only inspected a few vans. We went into the office to tell Carl that we had gotten an urgent call, and that we had to leave. We would be back tomorrow to finish up. It went as I expected. Carl shrugged, indicating he thought the whole endeavor was foolish, but never said anything that could land him in hot water.

We left to go find suitable paper and pen. I didn't like how this was going. We had just told a lie to the manager, that we had gotten an urgent call, when there was none. I silently chastised myself for not having made some perfunctory call to the office, ahead of going to see the manager. Then there would be a call record to corroborate my claim of an emergency, should it be investigated. But I was being paranoid, wasn't I? Why would anyone have reason to investigate anything I was doing? Still, I was leaving a trail, and it made me a bit uncomfortable.

And now we had to go buy paper and pen for the eighteen vans, and that would be yet another link to my activities. We felt it was better to buy them directly at a store, at a grocery. That way, there were so many people and so much economic activity that we would be more anonymous, even though there was no way to buy the goods without using digital dollars. That meant I was on record. As long as nobody looks, I am fine. If there is ever an investigation, there is enough to pin it on me. But this was no time to back out. I sent Ted back to the office so that he could not be implicated. Then I went to the store and bought the items.

Entry Twelve

Joe needed to know the plan. I think I have this part covered and untraceable. I had him brought back to the interrogation room. That was a little unusual at this point, but not unreasonable. I had made a two-page document for him. The second page was for him to sign, acknowledging that he had been given ample opportunity to confess and to accept Reeducation. But the first page contained his instructions. It told him the location of the pen and paper. It told him to write any details that might be significant. What was the trial like? How was he treated? Could he point out traceable landmarks? We weren't sure what questions to ask, so he would have to judge for himself. But his note should make no mention of why he was writing. Nothing to indicate he was trying to communicate to us. Joe read both pages carefully, and then signed.

On video, all that showed was Joe being handed a two-page document to sign. Entirely normal. He signed the second page, but only that document made it to the archives. That first page was shredded.

We had already been back to the lot. Before going in, I talked as I intended to always do, to Carl. We talked idle talk about his interests. He's into sports, so I'm suddenly into sports. And I causally found out what the inspection protocol is for the vans, without ever asking directly. I wasn't too surprised to find that they were lax. These weren't high security vehicles. They are mechanically maintained and cleaned after each trip, but the cleaning is for sanitary purposes, not security. I felt comfortable with our plan. We 'inspected' the vans, placing pen and paper in the armrest of each of them.

Now, all we could do is wait. I wondered how frequently we could inspect the vans without raising issues with Carl. I think I have him where I want him. He is afraid to cross me but still, I have an easy relationship with him.

I decided that the inspections would be irregular. If we did them on a schedule, they would become more of a presence in Carl's mind, and that might have consequences. Although it was accepted within my office that I should be doing the inspections, there was no written authorization. I felt that irregular inspections would be less likely to arouse any concerns that might make people in the office think twice. People examine schedules, but take lesser note of irregular activities. Anyway, Carl is glad to talk sports, so he's generally happy to see us. On an irregular basis, I will inspect once a week, on average.

Well, it only took a week! As we looked through the armrests, there was Joe's note! Written in cursive, of course. We both wanted to sit there and read on the spot, but we knew better. We checked the odometer. We completed the 'inspection', and casually said our goodbyes to Carl. But only minutes after that, as our car drove us back to the office, we voraciously read the note. Here's what it said:

"Trial was OK. Few questions, then sentence to Cancellation at the recommendation of the Prosecutor. Some sympathy, actually.

Taken directly to van after sentencing.

Past the Wall, it's mostly just fields and trees. Beautiful, really. Much better than inside. Seeing from a plane does not do it justice.

They took my watch. I don't know anything about the time or distance. I'll try to keep some track in my head, and tell you when I get there. Wherever there is.

It's been maybe an hour. Van is stopping. I see buildings a little in the distance. I must stop writing and get this into the armrest. Cancellation is fine with me, so far."

We both wished that we had learned more. But that was a lot! Checking our records, we found that the round trip was 248 miles. So, 124 miles one way, as far as we knew. There is something transformative in having succeeded at this much. Looking back, I see how predicable, preprogrammed, my life has been. Everything I've done, I've done in accordance with instructions, expectations and protocol. As I've looked back, I have to question how much of my life has been my own, and how much belonged to The System. I find little to distinguish between the two. But now, with taking the initiative to find people of my own kind, in finding ways to use The System to respond to my will, I am for the first time finding myself as an individual. I like it.

It's exciting to develop ideas and plans that aren't just reiterations of what I've been programmed to do. Of what to think. It's also distressing, to some extent. Creating your own answers, making your own way, is far more difficult than just following along. But it's the only way to find out who I am as an individual, and not just as part of The System. I see things now, that were never visible to me before.

I am no longer hesitant. I don't equivocate. I know I can't proclaim to myself or anyone that I am unquestionably in the right. But I will move ahead. I will do what it takes, whatever it is. I can't abide the mindless following of the Manifesto.

I don't want to feel safe. That's what it comes down to. I'm OK with an uncertain future, with having to make things work out based on my own efforts, and with no back-up from The System. No, I don't want to take foolish, pointless risks. I just want to live my life. My own life, come what may.

I know it's over with my bestie. How can I be the way I am, and live with them? I can't blame them for any of this. They are living the way they were taught, and they can't be bothered to question. They are happy with what they've got, and have no curiosity to find more, to comprehend more. I guess I sympathize with that. But I cannot live with that.

Entry Thirteen

Ted and I are contemplating our next move. We are encouraged by Joe, both in what he told us, and in that our plan worked. We could do much the same with other radicals, but to what end? We've discussed possibilities. It seems that we need a way for someone who has lived in the Wilderness to send a report back in the van. How could that be done? Joe had apparently met with no one as he left the van. What really did happen next? Did he walk to someplace, and people met with him? Good people? Bad people? My mind also wandered into Joe's description of the Wilderness as a hospitable place. People are willing to stay inside the Wall because they've been warned that it's dangerous out there beyond. I'm long past believing what I'm told, and I'm willing to go out into that Wilderness. But how to get there? It isn't just fear that keeps people inside, it is the Wall. It averages perhaps twenty feet. The real problem is that electronic surveillance makes it impossible to climb, or even get very close to, the wall without setting off alarms.

DHS has all the pertinent information about the Wall, but I can find no way to gain access to it. Honestly, it was only recently that I began to desire to go out there myself. Well, I have considered it for some time, but it is beginning to become a quest. Why does anyone even care if we go out? If someone wants to leave, why can't they just leave? The System. We have been educated throughout our lives about how essential and protective The System is. Now, I can see it only as an oppressive insult to my sense of freedom.

I thought once more of the books I've read. All the chaos and disagreement in the past looks better and better to me. I have no feeling in my heart that I am right, that my choices must be everyone's choices. I could understand having one point of view, while others have another. Is that so bad? And, at any rate, people weren't walled up in cities, back then. Mostly, they could go where they wanted, although I've seen the beginnings of this isolationism going back for centuries. History has been rewritten, borders redrawn, cities renamed and even moved. It is difficult to make all the connections, but I am seeing connections anyway. What Thought Leaders call freedom and democracy is just a ruse. Like a hamster running on its wheel, we feel like we are setting our own direction, but we're not. We are going nowhere. We keep busy at it, and pretend that that is the same as accomplishment. We are farm animals. We are somebody's pet.

I no longer just want to know what's out there, I *need* to know what's out there. I'm pretty sure that I need to live there. I find the uncertainty of what is out there to be more appealing than threatening. I will get there. I'm willing to die trying. That might be melodramatic; they don't execute people anymore.

It's plain that I can get into the Wilderness easily enough. I need only get myself Cancelled. Two things that bother me about that are that it would likely be found out that others were complicit with me. And somehow, it seems that while I would be asserting my independence, I would be doing it on the System's terms. I don't want to sneak out; I don't want to manipulate my way out. I want to walk out that gate when I choose, turn around and wave goodbye, and then go my own way from there.

Also, if I turn myself in or otherwise blow my cover, our entire scheme of pulling in believers would collapse. And they would not be Cancelled if the Thought Police discovered that it is what they want. What *would* they do? I could get out of that gate some way or another, but I don't want to leave my compatriots behind. I don't want to ruin it for them.

Use what works, I guess. After some consideration, we decided to select another radical and to get them to respond in the same manner as Joe. But we would instruct them to see if they could find a way to get information back to us after they'd experienced actual Cancellation. I wanted to pre-equip them with some means to do this, but I could only imagine possibilities. I came up with wild ideas, like having someone throw a note stuffed inside some sticky bag at the van as it returned, and hope it would stick. But could that work? At what point could they get close enough to do it, without being detected? The bag would be stuck to the outside of the van, and it most likely would be detected. I thought of some magnetic device that might stick to the metal parts, but it was no more realistic than the sticky bag.

As is the case sometimes, I guess, the answer put itself right in front of my face. I was reading an old magazine from 1952. I saw an article in the magazine about walkie-talkies. They were the precursor to today's phones. They were clunky and had few of the capabilities of today's phones. OK, they had *one* capability; you talk through them. But what hit me like a jolt, actually a day or two after I read the article, is that they are analog! Not digital, analog! A walkie-talkie signal would not be picked up by the Crawlers, because Crawlers only scan digital signals. Chances are, they would see an analog signal as nothing more than static.

I was sure I was onto something. I didn't even tell my compatriot. For now, at least, this was up to me. I had read that the signal on a walkie-talkie travels only a short distance, perhaps a mile depending on conditions. That was a problem, given that the vans drove the Cancellees apparently about 125 miles. Even if I could sneak a walkie-talkie into a van, what good would it do from 125 miles? I had no immediate answer, but it all played in my mind as a workable solution. If I could make it work.

Of course, the other part of the problem was, where do I get two walkie-talkies? I'd never seen one in my life. Could I make them? Perhaps, with time, if I studied how they worked, and could find the materials. That all seemed doubtful, so I went back to considering where I could get two of them. I decided I could go online. Everything is online, right? But I didn't want the Crawlers to get any ideas. So, I looked up things that are obliquely related to walkie-talkies. I started with military history. I did general research concerning armies and battles. Nothing that would be unusual for a history geek to study. And like almost anything online, there were ads, targeted ads. I looked at those ads. I found a few promising ones that featured old military equipment for sale. I was surprised to find out that one can still buy guns that way. Good luck finding any ammunition, though. I found two places in the city that sell the sort of items that might include walkie-talkies. Not surprisingly, they are both in the District. I knew where the one was, had walked past in on occasion. I gave it a try. I casually walked into the store, seeing multitudes of military artifacts, and in a case with knives and revolvers and such, were two walkie-talkies!

I had to suppress my pounding heart and not look obvious. I didn't immediately say anything to the owner about them. Instead, I wandered around, asking various questions about various items. There were other people there that were obvious regulars. They talked shop with the owner about various items, and about history that they all knew in common. It was quite educational, a history lesson in its own right. But I needed to get those walkie-talkies and I didn't need people wondering why I wanted them.

I acted like an interested neophyte in the presence of these experts. It didn't take much acting; I was genuinely interested, and a neophyte. Eventually I led the discussion to the walkie-talkies. What were they?

How did they work? Would they still work? Did they need some kind of cell tower? (I knew they didn't, but I wanted to appear entirely ignorant). The owner presumed they would work, but didn't have proper batteries. Nobody makes batteries like that anymore. Well, if they don't even work, would the owner lower the price? (I would have paid anything, but I didn't want to appear to have a need for them). The owner agreed to lower the price. Good.

I didn't want my digital purchase to show walkie-talkies, just in case I was audited. The good news is that there are no UPC labels on 150 year old walkie-talkies, and the owner entered the transaction simply as obsolete non-functioning military accessories. I couldn't help asking how he came up with that description and he said that's what he puts down for *all* of his goods. The other guys in the shop laughed. There was some sort of in joke going on there.

I chuckled along with them. Why not? I paid and started walking out of the store. One of the guys followed me out. He asked what I needed walkie-talkies for. I said I just thought they were neat looking and would look good on the shelf. He didn't seem convinced. That's when he told me that security system batteries could be made to power a walkie-talkie. I tried to appear only mildly curious. He explained that the walkie-talkies used twelve volt batteries. Security system batteries are three volts. So, four security system batteries in series would provide the twelve volts. He saw my interest, easily enough. Then he said it would be best to have groups of four batteries arranged in a parallel circuit to provide adequate power for a usable length of time. I said with a smile that it appeared that he had done that before. He gave the same chuckle that he gave back in the store. "A time or two," was his reply.

I knew enough about electric circuits to understand what he was saying, but I still felt it was beyond me. I asked more questions, with little pretense that I was putting these on my shelf. "Look," he said,

"I can do it for you. Get me twenty-four security system batteries, and I'll hook you up." I hesitated for a moment. I felt comfortable with this guy. He certainly hadn't been hanging around in that store just waiting for me to come along so he could fleece me. I trusted him, but what did he want in return? "Don't worry about it," he said. "Someday maybe you can help me out in some way." It was a weird feeling. My intellect told me to run, but I think I needed him more than he needed me. This would probably work out.

I got the batteries, although I was a little concerned that the Crawlers might wonder why I was buying 24 security system batteries. I met "John" at a designated place. He didn't want me to know where he lived, and the same for me. We trusted each other, but no need to take chances. We chatted about nothing special as he rigged the batteries into the appropriate groups and connected them to the walkie-talkies.

"Now, for the moment of truth," he said. "If we work them too close to each other, they'll squawk, and they might be damaged. I'll go down the street with one. You keep the other. It's on, so if it works, you'll hear me. To talk to me, you just push this button."

I saw him disappear around the corner and wondered if I'd ever see him or my walkie-talkie again. And then my walkie-talkie spoke to me.

"This is John. You there?"

I pushed the button. "I'm here."

He came back around the corner and handed me his walkie-talkie. "Looks like you're good to go," he said.

I asked how it was that he knew how to make them work.

"I've got a few skills," was his oblique answer.

I asked if there were many other walkie talkies out there. There was that chuckle again.

John is a guy I know I don't want to lose track of. It probably would have been safe to trade numbers, but John especially thought better of it. But we made arrangements to be able to contact each other.

Chip Kussmaul

Entry Fourteen

I didn't tell my compatriot about my discovery. Not right away. It's almost childish, but it's a secret that I want to relish. Besides, I'm still not sure what to do with the walkie talkies. Something else has been getting my attention anyway. We got a report of a radical in DHS. Perhaps more than one. That sort of thing just doesn't happen at DHS, and I don't know what to think. I've hoped to be able to gain information on Cancellation in some way from this office, and now I have a reason to go there. But initially I just need to do my job. I met with the Deputy Director of Compliance at DHS, in her office. It was an odd meeting. I wouldn't have expected a person in her position to contact me. I'd expect the agency to want to keep its investigations in-house and avoid publicity. I wasn't even sure what could be expected of me that she couldn't do herself.

It turns out that she just wanted to be out from under the situation. There appeared to be two factions within the Document Processing Department of the DHS. The two factions were accusing each other of sedition. They wanted each other Cancelled.

I caught on quickly enough. This was just office politics in a department full of clerks who had gotten worked up over who-knows-what. Maybe somebody was cheating with somebody else. I'd try to find out, if only to keep the peace. The Compliance head gave me security clearance and carte blanche to interrogate anyone I needed to, in order to sort things out and get this behind all of us. I could see why she wanted this handled outside of the DHS. Anything she did internally would be seen by somebody as favoritism. There was no way she could come out on top, no matter what she did. Except to punt it to me. She gave me the names of the principal instigators and I started with them. I'd meet with each of them in their own offices.

That tended to make them feel more relaxed, and relaxed people say more.

Sure enough, there was a love triangle going on. It took a little while to break through the veneer, but then the personal aggrievements started to come into play. I was thinking about how to cool this all down. I would probably recommend transferring at least one of the guilty parties to another department altogether. A few of them should have been fired, but that never happens. At any rate, I dutifully took the statements from both the principal parties and their allies, a total of twelve people.

But the eighth of those twelve made it all worthwhile. She gave her statement, her observations of who said what and when. She was more lucid and rational than most of the others. And, given that I was authorized by the Compliance Chief to do these interviews, she saw no reason to withhold classified documentation. I wasn't sure what to do with this, but I wasn't going to let the opportunity go by. I wanted to know what individual responsibilities each of the parties had. I didn't need to know, relative to the investigation; I wanted to know, because it might help me go fishing.

Most of the other parties had jobs that barely qualified as classified. They essentially collated information before it all got placed in files that probably no one would ever bother to look at again. But 'Sarah' worked in Cancellation. It turns out that she participated, ostensibly as a clerk, but she had input in forming Cancellation policy. She was perhaps in her early fifties and her records showed she had worked at DHS for nearly thirty years. She would know a few things.

I chatted her up. Cancellation must be an interesting department to work in, I suggested. She had no reason to be reticent, given my security clearance, so she talked freely. Before Cancellation, she said, there was continual chaos. People couldn't agree on much of anything. Hate speech was prevalent. Multiple internet sites sprang up that fostered the idea of total freedom to express any thought or idea. It became impossible for the government to control the narrative. People depend on the government not just for their physical security, but for their emotional security. People were becoming quite stressed, and something had to be done.

So, the DHS was authorized by the president to form a division to investigate the means to quell all the dissent. I knew the basics of all of this, but Sarah was giving me the inside view, in detail. First, she said, as usual, a study was made. And for that, there needed to be a committee to do the study, The Committee to Investigate Hate Speech. Sarah was a clerk for that committee.

Tell me more, I asked. Sarah said the committee made sense at first, as far as she was concerned. With all the dissention, marches, and even riots, something had to be done. With social media, large groups of dissenters could be summoned to appear at almost any time and any place. It was very disruptive to the Social Order.

But Sarah was bothered all along with the clear partisan nature of the study. Clear hate speech was considered constitutionally protected, if it supported the president and his people. But if people spoke against him, then the study found it to be punishable hate speech. Still, Sarah said, she was younger and less able to see a bigger picture. She was surrounded by experts, and who was she to question? So, mostly, she didn't question.

She was telling all this almost as if she were on a psychologist's couch, and that she was relating her life to me, the psychologist. But she caught herself: She was saying things that could be considered Cancellable. I told her sincerely that I only wanted insights and the truth, and that her statements were safe with me. It was a big ask. With where she was going, she could be in big trouble, even if I did have clearance. I think she really wanted to discuss this.

Sarah had never really felt good about what was happening. Sure, it seemed that something had to be done about the dissention. But it was quite clear that the dissent came from both sides, yet only the one side was ever accused of hate speech or violence. When entirely equivalent things happened on the other side, it was called anti-hate speech or "preserving democracy." Blatant crimes went not just unpunished, but uninvestigated.

The committee completed its study, after a number of years. No, it wasn't big news, eagerly awaited by the public. In fact, it got little notice. But then a committee was formed in Congress, the Hate Reduction Committee. They wanted to filter any and all online communications, allowing only content that they consider acceptable. The NSA had existed for years, and had access to essentially all communications, whether internet or phone. If it was digital communication, the NSA has a record of it. The committee wrote a bill, which became law, that the NSA would send any content that they felt violated the Hate Speech Laws to the DHS for consideration. And inside the DHS, the Cybersecurity and Information Security Agency (CISA) was formed. All for our own good, of course.

Sarah said that it started off slow, as these things always do. They didn't do anything too drastic. But, little by little, it intensified. Initially, Hate Sites were just shut down. Many Citizens complained at the shut-downs, but other Citizens were glad of it. But as fast as they shut down sites, other sites would spring up, so DHS instituted a policy of prosecuting the violators. First it was civil, but then it was criminal. Many things bothered Sarah about this, not least of all that DHS was writing its own laws and Congress made no effort to stop them. After a while, the NSA was combined into the DHS for greater efficiency.

Sarah said it was like that story about the frog in boiling water. There was no exact point where it all went wrong. But what seemed like a good, necessary idea ultimately morphed into top-heavy, top-down authoritarianism. Now, Sarah said, we all have to watch every word, and who we say it to, or we can be in trouble. Sure, it's only the worst cases that get Cancellation. But people can say the most innocuous things, and lose their job. Lose benefits. Lose their standing in the community. That's the worst part of it, Sarah observed: People have become so afraid of forming their own thoughts, that their own thoughts are now really the Thought Leader's thoughts. People seem afraid to even consider anything that goes outside the "walls" of The System. Conformity is king. Failure to conform, in thought, word and deed is now criminal.

Sarah had been looking off to the side the whole time, but then she turned to me. Her eyes pleaded with me.

"What have I done?" she asked. A tear came to her eye.

 I was never good at handling such things. "It certainly isn't your fault," I suggested. "What could you have done?"

"I don't know. I did do what I could to make the department more reasonable, but I could have done more."

"You could have done little. You're just a clerk… I don't mean that negatively, but there's only so much you could do." I was trying to be helpful, but perhaps I wasn't. "You know, there were clerks in the Nazi party. What could they have done? And perhaps many of them did as much as they could."

Sarah smiled a little. "Well, thanks for trying. I just can't believe it's like this." She paused and considered. "And, maybe it's not all bad. Nobody disagrees. No arguments, at least not about government. People like that the big decisions are made for them. Housing, healthcare, jobs, education, retirement; it's all automatic. No need to fret about what choice to make, when there are no choices. No need to get into political arguments, when there is only the one party. Just vote for them, so you are on record as being a supporter."

It was painful to me to see the look of resignation on her face. It was painful to see that there was nothing I could do. That we could do. I know from my books that, in the past, people in situations like this had choices. They could vote for different people. They could call or write their congressman and complain, without losing their job. They could march, and carry signs. How much good did any of that do? Did it really make things better? I don't know. But the freedom itself seems like a worthwhile goal. I have some perspective at this point: In these last few years I'm not more comfortable, I don't have more money, but I know better who I am than when I submitted to the Thought Leaders. And I need that. I need this.

I desperately wanted to know what Sarah could tell me about Cancellation. What it was and where it was. She might know little or nothing. Or maybe a lot. But I didn't want to press it right now. She might withdraw. Then again, giving her time might cause her to think better about the things she had said, and shut down anyway. But something in me said to let it go for now. I felt compassion for her situation. Maybe I would make a good psychologist. Anyway, I would get together with her another time to try to find out what she knew about Cancellation.

Entry Fifteen

Sarah and I trust each other. That can be dangerous, when you don't know a person well. Apart, even, from concern about honesty and integrity, two people can start out thinking they are compatible, and then have it all go to hell. Life is like that. My relationship with Riley is like that. I trust Sarah, but I can't know how it will go from here. If we confess too much to each other (who am I kidding; I have confessed nothing concerning my surreptitious activities), and then had a falling out, it could be hazardous.

I've kept the pointless he said/she said investigation open longer than it needs to be, so that I have good reason to continue to speak with Sarah. But, two concerns. I cannot justify the time I've spent interviewing her, even as legitimate as the investigation is on its face. Second, Sarah trusts me to a great extent, but I still haven't revealed what I know, and what I have been doing. I feel a bit duplicitous, but in a good way, I suppose. I certainly mean her no ill-will.

Sarah is no fool. She must know that my curiosity about Cancellation is a bit excessive relative to my having any professional reason to know. I think she wonders, but feels it's better to not ask, to not open doors that can't be closed.

At any rate, I feel it best to have at least a pretense that our conversations are part of an official investigation, not just for my sake, but also for hers. The façade of official investigation serves us, I think, both tactically and emotionally. Now that I think of it, it's still as if I'm her psychologist. She feels comfortable saying things to me, her psychologist, that she might never reveal to someone in a personal relationship.

But I couldn't keep meeting in her office. I was spending too much time, and people certainly noticed. With luck, they only thought I was hitting on her, and nothing more. And, OK, they wouldn't be entirely wrong about my being attracted to her.

It was at the Starbucks a few blocks from her office that I asked directly what she knew about the details of Cancellation. For both our sakes I didn't want to reveal any specifics concerning why I was asking, but at this point she had discerned a lot.

I'd made sure we were seated far away from others so that none would hear. And we both knew to not use the actual word "Cancellation" when anyone was within ear-shot. I was asking her to reveal information that she had never previously revealed to anyone. We were both walking a fine line. I wanted to press on gently. Otherwise, she might ultimately have thought better and held back.

I started conversationally, with matters that anyone was free to discuss. "You know, I'm still trying to figure out if Cancellation is a punishment or a reward." Sarah knew my point, but said nothing. "The two main choices for a defendant are Reeducation and Cancellation. The vast majority almost eagerly accept Reeducation. But those who refuse Reeducation readily accept Cancellation without even knowing what it entails, apart from that it means being vanned out of the city. Why would anyone do that?"

I had my own thoughts, but I wanted hers. I think, in this moment, Sarah concluded that I had motives beyond what I was telling her. And she decided to trust me on my motives, She was putting a lot on the line.

She said, "Well, I can tell you, Cancellation isn't as bad as people think. At least there is no painful or terrifying aspect to it. But that's all kept secret, so that people can imagine the worst. People fear the unknown, so if they don't know what it is, they fear it all the more. If they don't know what it is, they make up their own 'facts'. Besides, so many people want to be accepted. They want to conform to the norms. To be shunned by their own people is something they fear every bit as much as Cancellation. So, Reeducation is a perfect fit. They get to avoid the unknown that they have over-imagined, and they go through the Reeducation program that makes them once again acceptable to The System. It's almost like they've been cleansed, and can now hold their head high amongst their peers."

"Couldn't have said it better myself… In my prosecutions, I find that some people truly regret whatever it was that got them prosecuted. They feel guilty and they can assuage that guilt with the Reeducation program. But others, they're just playing the System. They have no regrets beyond having been caught. Both types are treated the same, get the same reeducation. I don't think The System even knows the difference. Or cares."

I continued my thought, "The people who choose Cancellation; they are the ones who are truly different. I guess they so dislike The System that they'll try anything, even that unknown that so many people are afraid of. They'll take Cancellation, rather than remain subjugated." Sarah made a good sounding board. I was working some of this out as I spoke.

Sarah smiled at me in a funny way. "That fits with anything that I know. I look back at thirty years of how it got to be this way, and I see that a large number of people, maybe most people, want to just get through life as easily and comfortably as possible. They want easy to learn answers to obvious questions. They really don't understand the concept of 'points of view'.-Over time, and a little too late, I began to realize that a lot of the people who want easy answers were taking charge of running our agencies. It was their nature to make simple answers a part of public policy. Little by little, dissent got weeded out. Challenging the policy, pointing out its obvious failings, was slowly extinguished. Now, look at us. We are bred and educated to conform. Nobody even asks why, anymore. Conformity is the goal. Pure and simple."

"Pure and simple," I echoed. We were this far into a very meaningful conversation and still I had not directly asked her what she knew about the specifics of Cancellation. It was time. "We both know that there are people who choose Cancellation without even knowing what it is…." I paused briefly, watching her expression. I think she anticipated my question; "You've told me it's not as bad as people think…So, what is it? What is Cancellation?"

I was glad that her expression displayed no unease. In any other situation, with any other person, she would likely have gotten up and left. Even reported them. But we still had that veneer of an official investigation, and I did have clearance to interview her. And Sarah was glad to have someone to talk to.

"I don't know everything, but I know the basics pretty well. After all, I'm just a clerk. Nothing hinges on me, but I read and hear a lot. Frankly, it's what I hear that counts, because not much of it is written down. Well, it is written down, but it's mostly BS. What's written down, as you know, talks about how a person who doesn't appreciate the teaching of the Thought Leaders and who refuses to work within The System must be expelled for the sake of The People. What's written is more about how heinous it is for someone to not go along, but little about what actually happens when they don't."

Sizzle and steak, I thought to myself.

She sipped her coffee. For effect? To gather thoughts? And she looked straight into my eyes, always a good sign. "Like everything else, it started slow. It was more about rationalizing than about planning. Or at least both together. I don't think I've ever seen any of my superiors contemplate the consequences of their actions. They just react to the issue. If it's bleeding, put a band-aid on it. Don't bother to ask what caused the bleeding."

Another sip of coffee, and she continued. "Too many people were expressing a desire to set their own direction in their own lives. Why not? I ask myself now. But it was seen as threatening at the time. There were no walls, then. Many people simply left and went to wherever. Nobody ever said it out loud, but I suspect that the Thought Leaders were concerned about the number of people leaving, as well as the number of people agitating for freedom within the city. The older I get, and the more I think about it; why couldn't they just leave people to make their own choices? But they wouldn't. They felt threatened. I think their own beliefs are so weak that they feel threatened by any challenge to those beliefs. Rather than defend their ideas intellectually, or even morally, they accuse the dissenters of treason, or whatever.

"The Wall was built to 'protect' us. From what, they never specifically said. It worked, I guess; we were never invaded. But of course it keeps us in every bit as well as it keeps others out. No problem; people were free to leave of their own accord. Until the gates were shut and then they weren't. The problem was, too many people had been leaving. So, they started regulating who could leave. And then they just stopped any pretense, and the Thought Leaders proclaimed that anyone who would want to leave this Utopia was a traitor. The Central Planning Committee made its rules, and the Thought Police enforced them. In short, that's how it got this way. That all won't show up in any history book taught in school today, but that's how it got this way."

Still, she hadn't said what she knew about Cancellation. I decided to wait her out. If I pushed, she might pull back. But, still looking straight at me, she continued.

"So, what is Cancellation, really? They drive the dissenters to a location a little over a hundred miles from here. They are free to do as they please and go where they wish, after that. But they are warned that if they come anywhere near the city walls, they will be picked up and 'bad' things will happen. I have no idea what those 'bad' things are. Anyway, to my knowledge, no one has tried to come back. By my best count, there have been well over a hundred thousand dissenters sent out. They've been supplied with tools and equipment and such, in order to build themselves their own town, or city, or whatever. They have plenty of room to grow their own food and provide for their own energy. But electronics are not allowed, although I've heard rumors that they have them anyway. I don't think it's an easy life, like we have here. But it seems that they're comfortable enough and happy enough. Honestly, from the talk I hear, they're happier there than we are here, and my superiors can't understand why."

We looked at each other. We both sipped from our coffee cups.

Chip Kussmaul

Entry Sixteen

It's our nature to see what we want to see. After Sarah told me what she knew, I started seeing the Cancellation city as a wonderful place. Fully free to do and say as you please. Associate with who you want, reject who you want. Even believe what you want, unfettered from the doctrine of the Thought Leaders. From what she said, that could all be true, but I don't really know.

I told my compatriot what I had learned, without telling how I knew. We feel much better about sending believers out for Cancellation, and do it more frequently, now. In fact, I want to go myself, but if I got myself Cancelled, as a Prosecutor who has gained some notice, the whole program might be drastically revised. That could make things worse for everybody.

They say a movement starts slowly, then happens all at once. I don't know how; I had told only my compatriot, but the believers came to know much of what I knew about Cancellation. Many of them now have started to *insist* on Cancellation! I want to accommodate them, but if I send too many to the Cancellation Courts in too quick succession, the Courts and the Thought Police will take notice. It's funny, in a way. Take notice of…What? These believers have little impact on the System and, indeed, if they go through with Cancellation, then they're gone for good. Over with. But The System doesn't so much act as react. It means to maintain the status quo, and they will react to anything that alters it, even if it's harmless, or even beneficial.

 As I thought about it, as I began to be able to see a larger view of The System, it made sense, in its own perverted way. The system is a well-oiled machine, all the parts working in harmonious synchronization. A few grains of sand can ruin that. Disharmony could wreck it.

People who don't like stress, and we are all trained to not like stress, recoil at changes that go outside their limited comprehension. I've begun to see the Thought Leaders not as great thinkers, but as tiresome meddlers of limited imagination and even less foresight. I don't need them! It took me most of a lifetime, but the more practiced I've become at making and evaluating my own observations, the less I need the Thought Leaders. And without them, why would I need the Central Planning Committee, the Thought Police, or The System?

It's all a house of cards. It's all there to provide an illusion. I've imagined what We the People would be like without any of this. Could we not still do our jobs and raise our families? What difference does any of this make? After a lifetime of not questioning, I ask myself why any of this exists, and realize it is all pointless. Are we sheep? Are we to be herded by sheep dogs and corralled at will by people who, I have found, are no smarter than the rest of us, know no more, and who are just as afraid as they have made the rest of us?

That's it! The people who rise to the top are the ones who most desperately need to control their environment. They can't abide diversity of ideas. They can't form a thought of their own, individually. So, they meet in committees and form group thoughts that satisfy them, and then force everyone else to comply, not for our sakes, but for *their*s. They are the ones who can't handle contradictory points of view. So, over time, they've taken control, and they've codified our existence down to the smallest detail. And it is not our physical actions that concern them so much as it is our thoughts. We are not to think our own thoughts; we are to accept *their* thoughts.

This is all so clear, looking back. But it's taken some time to get here. But here I am. I have hundreds of believers who *want* Cancellation,

87

while the Thought Leaders and The System have been touting Cancellation as the ultimate punishment. They should be willing to let them go, and be done with them. But the Thought Leaders cannot bear the thought that others might willingly choose different thoughts than theirs. It is threatening to them. Why? I don't know.

For at least the short term, I've decided to remand a slowly increasing number of believers to the Court for Cancellation, and see what reactions there are. As long as no one reacts, I can keep remanding more believers.

It helps to have Sarah on the inside. She doesn't know exactly what I'm up to, and doesn't want to know. But she's willing to help. It's funny how that works. She should have little useful information, being just a clerk. There are meetings of the Directors of CISA that she is excluded from, not having high enough clearance. But then they discuss those same issues with each other at lunch, right in front of her. So, I asked her to let me know if there was any unusual discussion going on concerning the increases in Cancellation.

It's odd, when I think of how this all began; me, just a guy who had doubts about The System. I was wandering in the dark, so to speak, questioning whether I was dysfunctional. Now, I know the System better than The System knows The System. I know that a lot of people have been playing along, thinking they have no choice. I know that too many people ask too few questions and accept way too much. I suppose that's a value judgement, and who am I to judge? But who are the Thought Police and the Courts to judge?

I need to be proactive. More proactive than I have been. Believers have been finding each other, communicating and deciding that they want to be Cancelled. Initially, I developed a means for them to be found and brought to me. Now, they are coming to me on their own, insisting on cancellation!

It just cannot remain like this. In my entire lifetime, The System has been largely an unyielding monolith. It continually gains mass and inertia to the point that there is no real movement at all. That is going to have to change, because the situation is changing. I knew that The System would develop no actual plan, relative to the ever-increasing number of believers, that they would merely react.

They would build more holding cells for believers. They would declare then mentally challenged and send them to institutions, where they could be forgotten. They would tighten down verbal communications, more Spies and more Crawlers. They might shut down my investigations. What they would *not* do is reexamine their approach to government. They would not reconsider what it means to be a citizen. They would *never* question their own authority.

That puts me at an advantage. They say, "Know thine enemy." I can't say that they are truly my enemy, but still, I know them. I understand them. They have no idea what a believer truly is. They can't even grasp the concept. So, we must think and act in ways that The System can't adequately react to. I've read in books about how battles, and even wars, have been won, not by superior power but by superior knowledge and comprehension of the realities. The Trojan Horse. It is legend, perhaps, not reality. But it is a parable that illustrates reality. Know thine enemy. We know them; they comprehend us not at all.

I haven't discussed these thoughts with others in my close circle just yet. Word gets out, for one thing. But I also want to be able to think my way through without excess distraction from others.

First, define the problem. The problem is that huge numbers of people are living artificial lives within The System, when they would rather be free. But other huge numbers of people like the way it is. My own bestie wants everything to stay the same. Can I insist that it all change, and force others to comply? Can others force me to comply with The System, with no other claim than it's 'always been this way'?

I've read in the books, there had always been slavery, until enough people decided to stop it. 'It's always been this way', is not an adequate reason for keeping it this way. So, the problem is, we have two main groups, and each wants something different than the other. In direct contradiction of each other. And the one group is in control. If only that group in control would just acknowledge that others want different lives, and let them have it.

Wait! They DID do that! That's what Cancellation really is. Let those others out and let them do their own thing. It was never really intended as punishment. Over time, the wall got built, and people could only come and go through the gates. The gates were generally open, but there were restrictions. And then restrictions got continually tighter. And the Thought Leaders taught that Cancellation was a punishment, that those sentenced to Cancellation would suffer from the danger, discomfort, and uncertainty. Over time, freedom came to be seen as a threat. Amazingly, the Thought Leaders taught that freedom was a threat to democracy. And they were believed!

In the past, there was a city, or part of a city, called East Berlin. It was walled off by their own Thought Leaders in much the same way as we are walled off today. And the citizens were told the same things. They were told that the wall was not to keep them in, but to keep criminals out. North Korea, which of course still flourishes, has done the same thing, but to the entire country. The irony is that, in my books, East Berlin and even North Korea are seen as totalitarian regimes that were bad for the people. While the walls around East Berlin were torn down in the 1990s, North Korea persevered and now has its own Thought Police and System. Most people don't know that history. It isn't taught in schools. I only know because I read the old books on my own.

There's an idea! Can we get people to read those books? Would they even care? Many would, but many would not. I know that the wall in East Germany was taken down because enough people had enough awareness of other choices to want to take it down and try freedom. My books say that many in East Berlin actually preferred the wall and felt disrupted by the changes that freedom brought on. It's true enough; freedom can be disruptive. If people can change their mind whenever they want, real, essential change could be permanent. I think I prefer that!

But anyway, let the people read the books. Many won't but some will. If enough do, it could lead to enough people seeking freedom so that we could tear down our own wall with impunity, just like the Berlin wall!

But how can enough people read those books? Online, all such books are banned by the Thought Police, and the Crawlers would find them in seconds. Wait! What if the books were handwritten in cursive? The Crawlers can't read cursive. Most programmers that program the Crawlers can't read cursive. We could publish cursive writing extensively, sending it out as JPEGs. The Crawlers would not recognize it as anything of concern. It could only last so long, before the Thought Police caught on and acted against it. I figure, in no time at all, Crawlers could be set to censor anything that looked like cursive, even if they couldn't read it. But if we could get a head start, it could work!

Chip Kussmaul

Entry Seventeen

I keep thinking about what could work. I don't think we can just feel our way through this. That's what the Thought Leaders do. We need to have plans that are well enough developed that they could be implemented swiftly, before The System could adequately react. I've read about guerrillas in my books. They are small military groups who plan attacks and execute them, before government forces can react. That really seems to fit, here, even though I have no expectation of great physical violence. I hope.

And when I think of military, and the ability to beat The System, I think of those guys at the military surplus store. I'm familiar with the people of the District, interact easily. But I don't know them well. I've had the sense, right from the start, that those military guys know people and know things that most of us are not aware of. I can't afford to be too trusting or assume too much, but I'd bet a lot that those guys would love to see The System taken down. They wouldn't be timid about it. And those guys know other guys…

I made an excuse for myself to go back to the store. I didn't think they'd remember me, but when I walked in, the owner greeted me with, "Hey, it's walkie-talkie guy!"

John turned to see me, as well as two other guys that I didn't recognize from before. There was a genuineness to the greeting that put me at ease. "I'm surprised you remember me."

"Oh, a shop like this mostly has regulars. So, when an unusual face appears, we remember…We even take note." And there were those chuckles.

"What notes did you take?" I felt comfortable, even without being sure what was unfolding.

"Sometimes a strange face appears here, and we need to check it out. Sometimes it's just a guy who wants a pair of walkie-talkies. Sometimes it's someone who is snooping. Sometimes it's a little of both."

I was being challenged, but not threatened. And I didn't appear to be threatening to them. "I do work for The System, but I'm not an Investigator. The office knows nothing about this, and I prefer to keep it that way. As for walkie-talkies, I was just intrigued as to whether that old technology could still work."

"Well, now you know," said John. "So, why are you back?"

Again, a challenge, but no hint of a threat. He was asking a legitimate question, and wanted a legitimate answer, no double speak. None of this was what I was used to, in a small store that should be full of "Good mornings," and "Have a nice days."

Interrogation is an important part of my work, but I wouldn't expect it in small retail shops. I was a bit flummoxed. They were entirely friendly, even welcoming, but they intended to know my intent. How much could I tell them? I wanted their support, but I knew nothing about them.

"I was wondering if walkie-talkies only work in pairs. It seems to me like any number of walkie-talkies could all work together."

"Well, yes, they could," said John. "Got a lot of friends?"

Again, the chuckles.

These guys could double-speak when they needed to. So, I said, "I've got some now, but I'd like to have more."

"Oh," said the owner. "Then you might want a ham radio set-up. It can have a longer range, much longer, and transmit to any receiver that's capable of receiving the signal. You could make a lot of friends that way."

"That sounds like a great idea. Is this something that people already do? I doubt I'd be the first, right?"

Perhaps that was a step too far. Their expressions stiffened a little. All of them. Whatever they really did here, they were all in on it.

 "I suppose other people have friends, not just you," said John. "And some friendships are kind of tight, and not quick to let outsiders in."

"But then how can that circle grow? You can't have too many friends."

I had them intrigued. We all seemed to have a sense that we could be helpful to each other, but no one wanted to tip their hand. The owner straightened a little, and looked me in the face. He was reading me. A person can lie with words, but it's difficult to lie with the eyes. Especially for a period of time. I let him regard me for as long as he cared to.

"You don't just work for The System. You are a Prosecutor. And you've been concentrating on prosecuting believers. Why?"

They had checked me out! Then again, I have achieved some notoriety at this point. Still holding his gaze, I replied, "I've found an easy way to find believers, and I've done it from right under my superior's noses. They pay me to do it! I wasn't sure, going in, what to expect. It's never been my intention to punish believers. But now that I've found so many of them, I'm not sure what to do with them. Cancellation seems to be desirable to believers, but if I send them all for Cancellation, the large numbers will be noticed by the System. And then, who knows?"

The owner didn't move his head, nor did I, but his eyes moved over to John for a moment, and then back to me. "Ever heard of Bre'r Rabbit?"

In fact, I had read about him in a book. And I recognized why he was asking. "Yes, there's a parable about him. Bre'r Rabbit lived in the briar patch. For most people, a briar patch is a horrible place, but for a rabbit, it's a good, safe place to live. The fox and the bear had been out to get him for years, and they finally did. They were deciding what horrible things they could do to Bre'r Rabbit, and Bre'r Rabbit told them, 'Do whatever you want. Burn me at the stake. Chop off my head. But please, *please*, don't throw me in the briar patch!' So, of course, that's exactly what they did. The rabbit, comfortable and safe in his briar patch, let out screams and groans as if he was suffering. That satisfied the fox and the bear, who had no idea that they'd been duped."

The owner again glanced at John, and then back at me. He put his hand on my shoulder. "Welcome to the briar patch!"

There were chuckles all around, including mine.

Chip Kussmaul

Entry Eighteen

Yes, answers inevitably lead to more questions. Look at all the answers that I now have! Only a few years ago I was a complacent citizen, going through the motions with little sense of a personal direction. I had a nagging sense of things, but knew little. The distinction, I guess, is that I knew that I knew little. Now, I know a lot. Now, I am my own man. Mostly. How different is anything as a result of my epiphany? Not that much. A significant number of people have been Cancelled, thanks to me. They are getting to have the lives they want, there in the briar patch.

But I still live in a city where people believe that the walls are for keeping people out, and don't even realize that they are being kept in. Sheep are like that, going where they are led, being corralled at will, and never questioning. I don't know that a sheep could have any better life than that, but I'm not a sheep. I want a life that I can own. That I can look back at and see a life that is distinctively mine, apart from the teachings of the Thought Leaders and of the direction of the Central Planning Committee. And I've had all I can take of The System.

Why doesn't everyone feel as I do? No, that's not my issue. People can want what they want. What concerns me is that so many people can't even recognize that they are nothing but sheep. Automatons, even. The Thought Leaders tell them what to think. This is no secret. Everybody knows that. Yet, they recapitulate the Thought Leaders's mandates as if they thought of them themselves. They willfully obey the Thought Police, and they wonder why there are those who don't. And those who don't obey need to be Reeducated for their own sake, as well as for the sake of humanity. Disagreement is seen as dangerous. I've come to see disagreement as a means for all of us to gain wisdom, gain intellectual depth. Anything I'm for, I can defend by using my own thoughts and reasoning. The same, for anything I am against.

And that is why my bestie has left me. The day was going to come. I don't blame them or fault them. Riley likes their life the way it is, uncomplicated, no real thought or contemplation required. Their 'discussions' with friends amount to nothing more than an exercise in confirmation bias. I used to be like that. Or at least mostly like that. I guess there was always that seed within me, and perhaps it was bound to grow. Maybe there's a seed in everyone, but the seed isn't always nurtured, so some wither and die. I remember Jesus saying something about casting seeds, and how some grow, and some don't.

I think I should feel worse than I do about losing Riley. But I don't. I find the freedom kind of refreshing. Funny thing is, it's not that I want to be free, free from relationships and obligations. I kind of crave that. It's just that I don't want to play a role, like in some video or something. A relationship should be full of discovery and growth, uncertain even. Yes, that's it! Some feel uncomfortable with uncertainty. They crave easy, obvious answers. And when the answers don't fit the situation, they try to force the situation to conform to their answers. And so, they experience nothing new. They do not grow. The seed withers and dies from lack of nourishment.

I not only accept the unknown, I crave it. I can only define myself, or attempt to, by experiencing challenges and finding out how I respond to them. Do I back away? Do I reject challenges as if they are a threat? Would I prefer to double down on my beliefs, rather than challenge them with new ideas and experiences? I like to think that the answer to all those questions is 'No." But maybe not. But I can always challenge myself, always weigh ideas, one against another, to see if I can find that which is essentially true.

I must not relent. I have come this far; I must keep going.

To date, I have found a means of communication that the System and the Crawlers are little aware of, and apparently unable to control. I have found that there are countless numbers of believers who want to be communicated with. I know there are people, even within The System who would like to bring it down. Surely, there has to be a way to do it. David v Goliath. Yes, David and Goliath! David didn't talk Goliath to death. He didn't run away from Goliath, and go live somewhere else, although he could have. David had developed a weapon, and the skillful use of it, such that he could kill Goliath with a single shot. I need to find that way. Escaping is not enough. Getting myself Cancelled, getting other believers Cancelled, is not enough. Is it?

Who am I to say? Who am I to decide? But then, who are the Thought Leaders to decide? My mind goes to Sarah. It often goes to Sarah. She has a great position in The System. She has worked there for nearly thirty years. My questions made her think, and her thinking made her question. She no longer blindly accepts The System. She has watched it become the rigid behemoth that it is. She has been a small part of making it that way, and now feels badly about it. You're supposed to feel good about what you build. You should be able to look back at where you came from, and be proud of what you've accomplished. Sarah looks back with regret. I wonder how many others are like her. How many others have just gone along, not wanted to rock the boat, didn't want to expend the effort, didn't want to lose friends?

It's like a wife in a bad marriage. Perhaps her husband starts drinking or doing drugs, and he ignores his responsibilities to her and ultimately even physically abuses her. It starts off good, and she is happy. But little by little, it goes to hell. But she has grown used to it. By degrees, one little step at a time, happiness turns to unhappiness. Content turns to discontent. But she is used to it. It's the way it is. Think of the emotional effort that it takes to break away and start over. And the husband is not likely to relent. Bad as her problems are, she will face bigger problems if she even hints that she wants to leave. So, she stays.

So, we stay. We are used to what we've got. We fear the change, we fear the effort and distress that is required to reestablish our freedom. Some people face that and manage to push their way through to the light. I am doing that, I think. Or am I just writing this to make myself feel like I'm accomplishing something? Writing is easy. Taking action is tough. Carrying through with this will cost me friends, my job, my career. What will I have afterwards that is better than what I've got now? My freedom! No, not some abstract sort of thing. My freedom! My ability to look at myself in the mirror and see someone who did not back down, did not prevaricate, did not accept the easy way. Did not just go along. I realize now, my freedom is worth more to me than a career, more to me even than my friends.

Entry Nineteen

I've been a little reluctant to bring together the people who are involved in this. If things fell apart, if there is an investigation, it's best if no one knows the other. Just like the Underground Railroad of the nineteenth century. Still, that being the case, all coordination has to go through me, or at least most of it. I've become a bottleneck in my own plan. My compatriot and I discussed this, in our double speaking way. We pretended to be talking about communication on a case. But we were discussing ourselves. He is getting eager to be Cancelled so that he can get out of here. But we both know that for an assistant prosecutor to get Cancelled would bring attention to the rest of us. I told him that I felt the same as he does, but there was nothing we could do, for now. I realize, though, that I can't just keep planning. I can't keep taking baby steps. There's an old saying, "He who hesitates is lost." Then again, "Fools rush in…"

Simply put, this effort needs to move forward, or it is in danger of collapse. I still haven't told my compatriot, or Sarah, about the military guys. Right now, they don't need to know. But I asked Ted what he thought he could do to break this undefined stalemate. Perhaps he should take some of his own actions and not rely on me. He said he belonged to a couple of Social Circles, and that he sensed that a number of people were closet believers. I told him he might want to pursue some of those leads, even create a new Social Circle, but be careful. Just one person reporting to the Thought Police, and everything could be shut down. We can survive some hits, if we remain loosely connected. So, for all I know, Ted is doing as we've discussed. It's best if I don't know.

Sarah and I have been seeing each other. On the record, I'm still 'investigating' the infamous 'he said/she said' incident. As with Ted, she and I have been discussing future plans, kept between ourselves. She is great as an inside source of activity at CISA. She has yet to see any indication that they suspect anything. Day to day activities and investigations don't make it to her department, but if a major trend was spotted, news of it would get to her. But by the time she knew, it could be too late.

We don't meet at her office too much. People would start to wonder. This time, we met at a different Starbucks. We don't want to be 'regulars' anywhere, such that people would remember. It was the Starbucks across from the gate where the Cancellation vans go. Why not?.

We sat outside on the patio. The 'bot brought us our coffees. Sarah absently stirred the coffee, giving it more attention than it needed. "My Mom has gone into hospice. She really didn't want to, you know, but it's gotten to be too much. After all these years, you'd think they could handle cancer."

"Sorry to hear that. I know what she means to you." It played in my mind that, while I was younger than her, I had already lost both my parents. She still had her mother, but she was going to lose her. Is it better that my parents were killed in an accident? As much of a shock as it was, I've wondered if there was the advantage that I didn't have to watch as they slowly, laboriously, died.

"It plays on me all the time," said Sarah. "I know it's her time, anyway. Even if she was healthy, she's getting toward the time of voluntary termination. But I wish she could have a full, comfortable life until then. They can make it so she feels little pain, but then she's not really Mom. She tries to handle the pain, so that we can really communicate, be together. I feel a bit guilty. I think she mostly does it for me. I'm a grown woman. She needs to make her own choices."

"She does, it seems." Gently I said, "Don't presume that her choices should be the ones that you want for her to make. Accept her choices."

Sarah smiled with resignation. "Her last days should be comfortable." More stirring of the coffee. "I don't want memories of her suffering."

"Life is like that. We like to think it's all under control. It isn't. No matter the technology and conveniences, life is never fully under control. That's why we can call it life, and not existence. Life. You do your best. People think they can engineer out the hard parts. I think, even if they could, they shouldn't."

Sarah reached the short distance across the table to take my hand. It was the first time we'd ever touched. "Even when I disagree with you, I like you."

"Disagree?"

"Well, I know what you're saying, but it's not your mother who is dying in pain."

The rebuke was mild, but still it stung. "I wouldn't hurt you. If I'm not helping, I'll just shut up about it."

"No, it's good to talk. The people in the office express sympathy, but no one really has anything to say. Sometimes, I feel alone, even when there are people, and they are sympathetic. You and I talk, and the talking means a lot."

And that meant a lot, to me. After a while, the hand holding became awkward and she withdrew it. But the sentiment remained. We were silent for a bit, and it was comfortable.

As if on cue, a Cancellation van arrived at the gate. There was a guard at the gate, as there was always at all the gates. The gate opened, without any action by the guard. It was evident that the auto-van could control the gate. There's nothing unusual about that, but it led to an epiphany of sorts; if the guard was there to defend the gate from outside intruders while the gate was open, why was he on the inside? No, he was there to keep us from getting out. There need be no law, no sign posted; subliminally every citizen gets the message. Stay inside.

As the van passed through the open gate, I saw countryside beyond. I wanted to be there. Whatever challenges the Wilderness presented, I wanted to be there. Sarah followed my gaze, knew what I was thinking. We watched the gate close tight.

After a moment, as we continued to watch the gate, she said, "Well, I know why we're really here." I felt her head turn toward mine, even as I continued to regard the gate. "What would you like to know?"

I took a moment, then turned my gaze to her. I wanted her to understand that our meetings weren't strictly business, so I didn't just jump in, but then, "I think we're reaching a critical mass, concerning certain matters. We can't expect to keep flying under the radar. Have you still heard nothing from the brass?"

"No. Every day is pretty much the same"

"Well, that's good. But I think that by the time you do hear something, it might already be too late. They say the best defense is a good offense. I think it's about time for the next step. I'm just not sure what that is!"

"I've had a thought about that. There's a bit of a weak link in the CISA system. We get reports all the time, of course. Most are handled at the lower levels and don't amount to much. But anything that needs the attention of the top brass is forwarded to the department for proper disposition to the proper official. Guess who makes that proper disposition."

I smiled. "Surely, it can't be that easy."

"It's not, entirely. I could hold back the reporting for a while, perhaps a week or two. Even a month, if I was lucky. But they'd catch on, and I'd be out of there. So, whatever you come up with, I could buy you some time. And I could let you know what's coming through. But the bigger it is, whatever it is, the less I'll be able to hold it back."

This was all good to know, but I couldn't know right now what use it might end up being. I did see that I would need to know immediately if anything of significance came across her screen. "If you see something, could you call me immediately? Make it about your mother. Telling me about her condition will be the signal. Serious, not too serious, and so forth."

"But, what if I'm really calling about my Mom?"

I thought for a moment. "If it's your mom, refer to her as Mom. Otherwise, say 'mother'."

Entry Twenty

It turns out that the military guys have been ahead of me in some ways. John won't tell me how many there are or too many of the details, for good reason. What I don't need to know, I don't want to know. Still, we have to plan. And it seems that John is better at the planning than I am. At least he appears to have been doing it longer.

He was explaining ham radios. He had one on the desk in front of us.

"You can talk, almost like on a phone. Or you can send Morse Code. There's advantages either way. Almost no one knows Morse Code, except for our guys, so it's almost like secret code. And the radios are analog, not digital, so the Crawlers aren't likely to recognize it as a significant signal. On the other hand, if the Thought Police catch on, they could program the Crawlers to seek analog Morse Code. Since we would be nearly the only ones using it, we'd stick out like a sore thumb. Still, it could be a long time before the Thought Police even caught on, and then perhaps weeks to convert the Crawlers."

John continued. "If we talk, rather than Morse code, then they can of course directly hear us. But would they? Almost nobody does analog anymore. Just like the Thought Police can't be bothered with all those books you've been reading, they can't be bothered with analog. I think it's their Achilles heel. You know, all this eavesdropping technology is created by tech geeks. It's their thing. They don't get their rocks off by chasing after books, or by listening to mostly dead-air analog signals. They could do it, but they don't want to. The government is never as smart as people tend to believe. And the people most unaware of that fact are the people in government." He grinned a little. "Present company excepted, of course."

I knew he was right about government. So many people, so little comprehension. They are their own self-fulfilling prophecy. I felt that if we got a good head start, we could crash The System before it knew what hit it. "From what you're saying, it seems that we only need one or two transmitters, but we need all the receivers we can get."

"Yeah," said John. "Today's communications are all two way. Even a TV communicates back to the Cloud about who is watching what. The System, CISA specifically, knows who's watching what, who's talking to who, all the time. They count on algorithms to spot undesirable trends. They've been throttling trends for decades. The average person isn't even aware that they are only getting the information that the Thought Police want them to get.

"Now, think of the old days. TV and radio stations broadcast their signal. It went in all directions, and any receiver in range, be it a radio or TV receiver, could catch the signal. But here's the thing, the broadcasters had no way of knowing who, or how many people were receiving the signal. There's no way to track it. If we broadcast by ham radio, the government might find it, but there is no way to find the receivers. Receivers only receive, they don't transmit. No fancy technology of any kind, digital or analog, can find the receivers. Think about it!"

"I'm thinking," I smiled. "It seems like we need a lot of receivers!"

"That we do," said John. "And that's a problem. They can be hand wired, just like the old days, but it takes time, and it takes parts that are hard to find. But we're working on it."

"How far have you come?"

"You don't need to know. We're working on it."

"Fair enough," I said. "So, at some point, we can communicate instantly with a large number of people. Just right off, I'm excited that no 'disinformation agency' can censor us. Hell, these days we have to watch what we say and where we say it, just in a conversation. Being able to speak at will to a large number of people, and the government can't stop us, is downright exciting. One little question…"

"What?" asked John.

"What do we say?"

John chuckled that chuckle. "I was figuring on you working that one out."

Then I had an epiphany. "Are you aware of a thing they called the Iron Curtain, back about a hundred years ago?"

"Of course," answered John.

"Radio Free Europe was created to send signals, just like we're talking about, over the Iron Curtain and into East Berlin and all the totalitarian countries. It took years, but Radio Free Europe had a lot to do with the overthrow of the totalitarian governments. In the end, it didn't take an army, it took an informed public. We need to do that now! I've been trying to find a way to communicate from within, but it would be only a matter of time before we were caught. If we could transmit from outside, and since the receivers on the inside couldn't be located, we could take down The System with plain communication."

"Sounds like a great plan. But Radio Free Europe had the backing of entire countries. We don't have that. Even on the outside, we can't be sure we wouldn't be caught and shut down. And I'm not sure how we get transmitters out there. Everything, in and out, is radio-traced for contraband. And for that matter, if we get a transmitter or two out there, who will operate them? And, sooner or later, the Thought Police will catch on and try to stop us."

I was a little upset at John. I had never seen him act doubtful. "We've come this far. Both of us. All of us, however many that is. This is our best shot. And it's worked before. We can do it again."

John pondered briefly. "I decided a long time ago that there is no sacrifice I wouldn't make for this. But being stupid, planning poorly, is not sacrifice. It is pointless martyrdom."

He was right. I still thought that we were developing a good plan. But we couldn't just jump in. "Well, be the devil's advocate. What am I getting wrong? What needs to be worked out?"

"I think we can get transmitters out somehow. I just don't know how. Yet. And even though receivers can't be tracked, transmitters can. Once the Thought Police caught on, they'd locate us in no time. We'd need to be portable, to keep moving. I don't see a foolproof way to do any of this. If we can stay ahead of them for long enough, it could work…But, I have a question for you; If we do all this transmitting, can we count on people to listen? Can we count on them to respond?

"I'm not sure what we can reasonably expect," I pondered. "If we provide the opportunity, the rest is up to them. I think I can live with that. Going day after day with no choices is more than I can take. But if freedom is offered to them, and they decline it, then I guess that's that."

Those words did not satisfy John. OK, they didn't satisfy me, either. But, just as John was being realistic about technology and strategy, I was being realistic about people. And, thinking of technology, I had a concern about one way communication. If we had a transmitter in the Wilderness transmitting, how would the people out there know what effect they were having? Moment by moment, how would they know what information to transmit, if things were to develop rapidly?

I expressed my concern to John. "We need two-way communication. Some way to get information out to the transmitters, so they can broadcast it back in. This won't work if it's only one way. What about the walkie-talkies? With such short range, can they be of any use?"

John saw my point, easily enough. "Walkie-talkies might be useful in the same way that you still need infantry, even when you have tanks. Infantry can go where tanks can't go. And infantry is more mobile and easier to hide. But a soldier can't be as effective as a tank. In theory anyway, we need both. No, not the tanks and soldiers," he laughed, "the Walkie-talkies and ham outfits. Just right now, though, I don't have it worked out. Let me work on how we can get the most thorough and reliable penetration with the communications."

We talked a bit more of the technology and how to best implement it. But that made me more aware of my own responsibilities. I need to get people in place. I need to do a full frontal assault on…ideology. I need to organize the people who want the freedom to think and express their thoughts, and to get them focused in mass numbers on taking down the Wall and rendering The System impotent.

On the face of it, it all seems impossible. But it has been done before. By the time citizens in Germany rose up against the Berlin Wall, the government system had collapsed of its own top-heavy weight. There was little violence. The People simply rebelled against the tyranny, and magically, the tyranny disappeared, disintegrated. Is it always that way? If enough people simply proclaim "Enough!" will any system topple? It seems so unlikely, yet I believe it to be true.

Chip Kussmaul

Entry Twenty-One

I feel comfortable counting on John to be able supply radios, receivers and walkie-talkies. It's up to me to decide how to use them. There would have to be people in the Wilderness that know the plan and could do their part. Cancelling John's people and getting them out there is no problem. Communication is the problem. Indeed, communication has always been the problem.. Censorship seemed so acceptable to me a few years ago. Now, well, it pisses me off.

I know now that a significant number of government workers, not unlike Sarah and my compatriots, are believers, and can be counted on to do whatever it takes, once we go into action. Others, of course, will not. I think of my bestie, and how we have split. There's been some animosity, from both of us, but not as bad as might have been. I don't know if that's because we saw it coming and were anticipating giving up, or if it's in our nature to roll with the punches. But I extrapolate; I think of all the people, all the relationships that will be tested in light of the coming dissent. That, too, was inherent in the break-down of the Berlin Wall. In the end, many in East Germany did not like having their lives disrupted by…well, by freedom. Freedom, I can see, can be threatening in a way. When you have no choice, the choices are easy to make. When the choices are near limitless, they can be daunting. And a free person can't blame the government for their own unfortunate choices. Having the government for a scapegoat can be comforting.

But we have to do this. We have the right to do this. We have the responsibility to do this. We cannot be expected to continue to conform just because others don't want to have to take charge of their own life.

I think the first step is to get people to not be so trusting of The System. That will be a hard sell for some. But if they doubt, even a little, that will drive a wedge. They will be more receptive to the other things we say. They will be more receptive to…the rebels. We are the rebels! I never thought about it, but that's what we are. How strange; insisting on our own freedom makes us rebels. Is that always the way it works?

Besides my own experience, Sarah is my best source for information that could be injurious to the status of The System. I think back again, to a time when old systems were always under attack, when people could say as they please, and the systems had to always justify and defend themselves. Not surprisingly, systems came and went and morphed, as people's opinions changed. We need that! We need that freedom of choice.

So, Sarah. She knows things, things that seem innocuous when they are a daily occurrence. But if we expose them in a new light, people might see by that light. They might not like what they see. I arranged another meeting with Sarah. At a different Starbucks.

"How's things at DHS, these days; at CISA?" Surely an innocuous question.

"Things seem about the same. We're pretty much handling the usual cases. Terror speech, misinformation, hate speech. The usual." She smiled a bit. In other words, our plan was still flying under the radar.

"Good to hear. I like to see the administrative state humming along like clockwork." I also smiled. She waited to find out what was next. "I've been wondering, who makes the decisions concerning what is hate speech, and what is just a contrary opinion? What is a 'terrorist' threat'? If two guys get into it over a girlfriend and one threatens the other, is that a terroristic threat? Is it hate speech? Is it misinformation?" I laughed at that last one.

Sarah looked at me a bit quizzically. She wasn't sure if I wanted inside information or was just bantering. And after all, the 'investigation' that brought us together was ostensibly about a 'he said/she said' incident. I arched my eyebrows a bit, and she understood.

"It's up to the Thought Police. They make the report and the recommendation. We pretty much go with what they say."

That's how it is in my department, although my department doesn't get into 'national security'. We handle plain old-fashioned local crime. It was funny, now that I thought about it; the actions, the words, could be about the same, but if CISA handled it, a person was in much bigger trouble than when my department handled it. 'Hate speech', 'terroristic threats', etc. were in fact generally not a lot different than when plain folks just got into it with each other.

"Do any of your superiors ever express thoughts contrary to Thought Police recommendations?"

"Not usually." She was about to leave it at that, but then, "Although I know of a few times when a Central Planning Committee member, or someone they know, got arrested. You can see the emails and texts going back and forth, and then the charges are dropped."

"Every time?"

"Every time. When it happens, you just let it go. You know? It's the way it is. But now that you ask, it sucks. It does seem that there are two justice systems; one for the people who run The System, and one for everyone else. You know, not that I've ever needed to worry about it, but if I'd ever gotten in trouble, things would probably have been taken care of for me. But it's not right. Just because it works to my advantage, doesn't make it right!"

"No, and that's not how they advertise. The Thought Leaders assure us constantly that we are equal, and treated equally."

"Yeah, they sure do say that."

We contemplated our words for a moment. "What do you suppose would happen if people found out about these sorts of things? What if they began to suspect that The System was full of corruption?"

"And how would people ever find that out?" she asked. Again, my eyebrows arched. I think Sarah was evaluating how much deeper she was getting, beyond what she had initially anticipated. But she seemed all-in. I watched her think. "They get pretty sloppy. They've had decades of being in full control, unchallenged. Just off the top of my head, I could come up with a lot, documented in e-files. If I spent a little time, I could come up with more."

"I've been thinking along those lines," I said. "Looking back, I see things that I didn't notice at the time, in my department."

"Well, great. And then what? Then we just send it all out in emails, and the Crawlers never notice? If you're trying to get the information out to the public, that's nearly impossible.

My eyebrows arched once again. "You leave that to me."

Chip Kussmaul

Entry Twenty-Two

I told Ted the basics of my intentions, without revealing plans. His work had brought him closer to the people I wanted to implicate. He saw little problem in getting e-files implicating some well-known figures. Then he hit me with the bombshell: Two of the Thought Leaders were involved in a kickback scheme to defraud The System. It was much as it was with Sarah; they were so used to doing it, they saw little need to be surreptitious. Ted already had an e-file with pertinent information.

 "What?!" I asked. "And you never even told me!"

"You never needed to know. And now that you know, what can you do with it? You can't prosecute them, because the courts will never allow prosecution of a Thought Leader."

"But think if everyone knew about it."

"So, are you going to go knock on doors and tell them one at a time? You can't put it on the web; the Crawlers will grab it in a moment."

"There might be other ways. I think there might be enough out there to really shake people's confidence, if they knew about it. And I think I can get it out to them."

Ted wanted to know how, but he knew better than to ask. "Well, if that's the case, I think I can get quite a bit. There's stuff out there that nobody talks about, but a lot of people know."

"Documented?"

"Yeah, documented."

I felt stupid that we hadn't had this conversation earlier. Much earlier. But, when things are the way they are for years and decades, you stop noticing, even when they're right in front of you. We wanted our freedom from these people, and never stopped to realize how well armed we were to claim that freedom.

It would take a little time. But not too much, I didn't think, for various people to organize and document what we knew. I haven't let on to the others, but I don't have full confidence that it will make enough difference. I've even had the sick thought that, if we do this and fail, the restrictions would then be made still tighter and more unbearable. I might still be Cancelled, as well as others, but the majority would not be Cancelled. They would pay the price. For that matter, Cancellation might be cancelled. And replaced with who knows what?

I have to try to make this work the first time. There's little likelihood of a second chance.

It sure couldn't hurt, and it might help, to study the history of such events. It's exceedingly ironic that, while the Crawlers have made it impossible to find useful information about revolutions online, there is no shortage of books and magazines full of useful content.

I came across "The Radicalism of the American Revolution" by Gordon Wood. We've always been told that the old founders of the former USA were racist colonizers. That's true, only to a degree. After all, these founders had been born in North America, as had been their parents and grandparents, going back for well over a century. They weren't colonizers, they were as natural born as the Indians. It's an interesting book. These men, that we have been told were stodgy, selfish people, gave up much, that we could all have freedom. They were, in fact, radicals just as I apparently am. They weren't perfect, they weren't clairvoyant, any more than I am. But I look at our

Thought Leaders, and I look at those founding fathers, and my heart is with the founding fathers.

And there's "The American Revolution in Indian Country," by Colin Calloway. What really got me thinking is that there were a number of different perspectives, all going on at once. Today, we are told that there is only one correct point of view, the Thought Leader's point of view. Any other point of view is to be considered subversive, and must be censored. Right here, in this book, a fair examination of different people, their points of view, and their lifestyles are given equal treatment. I want it to be like this NOW! I don't have to feel like I'm right, or that anybody is wrong. I just want my freedom to *think* about it!

"A Fool's Errand," by Albion Tourgee. Wow! It's like a veil was lifted. Of course, the Old USA had a civil war about slavery. But the way we are taught, you'd think both sides were fighting to keep the slaves enslaved. Of course, one side fought to free the slaves, and then tried to get them complete equal rights. I never heard *that* in any history class.

"Inheriting a Revolution," by Joyce Appleby. It's about the second generation *after* the American revolution. These people, and the lives they lived, and that *includes* blacks, is nothing like what they teach in history class. And, again, they thought for themselves, instead of having Thought Leaders.

"American Nations," by Colin Woodard. It turns out that the Old USA was made up of many distinct cultures, and that they never all thought the same or wanted the same. When I read a book like this, and then I think about how our Thought Leaders keep stressing 'diversity' when they really want us to all be the same, I know my cause is right. We must free ourselves from the ultimate tyranny, not against our bodies, but against our minds!

Where would I be without these books, and others like them? What would I know? The funny thing is, I and people like me are called 'believers'. But no, the people who blindly follow the Thought Leaders are the believers. They believe what they are told, unquestioningly. They don't want to gain greater comprehension and to individualize themselves through diversity of knowledge and perspective. They all want to be the same, and to believe the same. People like me are not believers, we are questioners. No matter how much we learn, we want to know more, comprehend more. All answers are springboards for other questions. It never ends. I don't want it to ever end. When I think that most people have never read even one of these books, I am appalled. I wonder how many of our Thought Leaders have read any books.

I can't let it stay like this. There is no sacrifice I won't make, nothing that I won't suffer, to have true diversity. I think about Starbucks. I imagine conversations such as must have happened in times past, maybe in the very buildings that Sarah and I have visited, when people, two people or a group, might sit there in public and argue about whatever they wanted!   They sat there and argued, in public, about political candidates!   And they had an actual choice! They could argue about economics or education or absolutely anything. But now, that's all hate speech and misinformation. There is only one right answer to anything, and that is the Thought Leaders' answer.

And now I know, The Thought Leaders don't believe their own Thoughts. They insist that we believe them, but they don't believe themselves. I've come repeatedly across a term that no one says today: Hypocrite. It's when someone says one thing but is thinking something else. It's when someone expects others to be honest but isn't honest themselves. It is The System. I see, ever more clearly, it is The System.

Chip Kussmaul

Entry Twenty-Three

I vacillate, between what to tell The People, and how to present it to them. One means nothing without the other. There has been no challenge to The System for as long as I can remember. How could there be? The System controls all information. How will people react to The System being challenged? Where I always want to know as much truth as possible, I have seen in my bestie and others that they want easy, comfortable answers. They don't want choices. They don't want to make decisions. They want it all pre-planned for them, so that life will be less stressful. What will happen when they face a barrage of information that challenges their belief system? It occurs to me that the people who already doubt, but have remained silent, will jump into action. But those who don't want to stress will reject the information, deny it, perhaps even rush to defend The System.

This could get ugly. It seems so tranquil now. All the media agree on everything, because they are really the same media, reporting from the same press releases compiled by the same System Influencers. What will happen when there is a competing news source, us, that blows holes through all the established propaganda.? Yes, it's tranquil, now. But it's phony. It's manufactured. It is the tranquility of compliant sheep, not of thinking human beings.

I vacillate, and right now, it's not about what to tell The People, but how. We can get the radios. I trust John in that. But where do we put them? How do we protect them? That's why we have to get the transmitters on the outside. They'll be in jeopardy even in the Wilderness, but they are sitting ducks inside the walls.

John knows some things that would be helpful, but is reluctant to say. I can appreciate his caution, but we need to get transmitters past those walls.

We found a place to meet.

"I don't want to know everything." I said. "In fact, the less I know about what you're doing, the better. Or at least, HOW you do it. But the transmitters have to get outside the Wall, and I can't seem to find a way. Pardon my being presumptuous, but you seem to have a way to get the parts you need. I don't need to know how, but can you get in and out past the Wall, without going through Customs?"

John considered a moment. "I suppose the Wall isn't entirely airtight. It's only twenty feet high. I remember a guy said once, 'show me a twenty foot wall, and I'll show you a twenty one foot ladder'"

I smiled. "But is there an invisible ladder that no one sees when you put it against the wall? Otherwise, I don't think that ladder works."

"OK, I was speaking euphemistically. But it occurs to me that it is possible to get through the Wall. Here's a thought: Transmitters are fairly big, and recognizable. If someone were to try to smuggle one through, and it was caught, the Thought Police could figure out a lot as to what it was going to be used for. But a transmitter is made of much smaller component parts, easier to smuggle, and if found, they give no indication of what they were to be used for. Then, use those parts to build the transmitters on the outside. I'd even throw in some pointless parts, to throw off investigators if they found them and tried to figure out what they're for."

Well, of course! "I don't want to know what I don't need to know. But is it possible to do this? Has it been done?"

"My intuition says 'yes'"

119

I was silent, as I considered the possibilities. Think of what we could know and what we could do, if we could communicate freely with the people in the Wilderness. If the Wilderness was in fact a nice enough place to be, and people were happy there, and The People were made aware, it blows holes through The System's assertion that Cancellation is the ultimate punishment. We have all been allowed to believe that Cancelled people languish for the remainder of their pathetic lives, regretting what they had done, and wishing they could be back with us, in the comfort and security inside the Wall. If the people out there were happy, and didn't want to come back, The People would have to question. I think I need that wedge. I need something that will cause people to question. If they are like me, once they start to question, they will not stop.

All that thought in the space of a few seconds, as I worked on a plan with John. "So, somehow, transmitters can be in the Wilderness and operational. And receivers can be in various places inside, and nobody would even know. Is that about right?"

"I'd say so. And with a little luck, the communications could go on for some indefinite amount of time, before the Thought Police even caught on."

"All we need is one or two people on the outside who can do this," I thought out loud. "They would need to build a transmitter out of those parts, and then operate them. They would have to keep moving them, and keep them powered. Any ideas?"

"Sure. I imagine there's a fair number of people who could do that. But it's one thing to get small parts to the outside; people are more of a problem. We couldn't count on successfully smuggling a person out."

"I don't see any need to smuggle them, I can Cancel them.

I had the thought of trying to smuggle parts in the vans, but it was fairly high risk. And if they were discovered in a van, it would all lead back to me. John said he had a way to get the parts out, so I would leave it to him.

I asked, "So, how long do you think it would take to get all the equipment together? I may be ready fairly soon to move ahead on my end. What about you?"

"I think a month. We've been prepping for a day like this. But now we have to focus on the specific plan. I think a month, maybe less."

My heart wants it to be tomorrow. But this all has to be worked out in my head, not my heart. I will make my plans to execute one month from now. Hell, I might need every bit of that month. Developing resolve is easier than acting on it.

John has two people that he wants me to cancel. That's not a problem, but it will take time, so I'm glad to have that month. I'll need to create a case for Cancellation of the two. I can't just declare that a person needs to be Cancelled, without a case. But it helps when the defendants are entirely cooperative! John will let me know when he has his two people ready.

Chip Kussmaul

Entry Twenty-Four

It's getting tense, now. It's to be expected. We've taken some risks previously, but most of anything we've done or said is defensible, for the most part. Even if we were investigated, it would yield little. There are no records that can't be explained, no meetings that weren't justifiable. All that must change, now. Sarah, Ted, Mary, and others are turning over records that we are not supposed to have. Damaging records. If caught now, it would be evident what we are up to. And that just makes me more pissed off. What are we up to? We are up to reporting the truth, factually and honestly. Why should we have to cover our tracks over that?

Once again, Sarah and I were at a Starbucks. The tension is playing on me, but it's up to me to keep things cool and under control. As under control as they can be, anyway. I looked over at Sarah. She looked more attractive to me than ever. Not all physical, but that, too. But also, I guess our commitment to this cause bleeds into our feeling of commitment to each other. Well, I'm assuming something; she has made no personal commitment to me. It's best that we hold off for now.

Sarah reached across the table and gave me a small gift box. I opened it. I turned my eyes up to her. She smiled coyly. Are we lovers or conspirators? I opened the box. I understood what this gift was, and left it in the box, out of sight of the others in the shop. It was an old fashioned flash drive. I knew there was no way the records that were on it could be safely sent online.

Her face expressed multiple feelings. "What's on here, it could only have come from me. It would take some time and back-tracking, but

I'm the only one that could have compiled all those files. Do not let this flash drive fall into the wrong hands."

"You can be sure I won't." I couldn't be totally confident in the immediate future, but this was no time to equivocate. "I appreciate what you are doing. We're all taking risks, but they're worth it. Our numbers keep growing, beyond anything I could have anticipated. I used to think there were only three of us. Personally, there is nothing they can do to me that would make me regret my actions. But I wouldn't want anything to happen to you."

Sarah calmed a little, less tense. "When you get down to it, I'm all in, no matter what. This has all developed slowly, little by little." She smiled hopefully. "At first, we weren't doing anything that was all that wrong. We could pretend it was innocent enough. If we'd been caught, some reasonable excuses would have gotten us by. Maybe some Reeducation!" We both laughed. "Don't worry about me," Sarah continued. "It's a choice for me, and I've made that choice. Wherever it goes from here, I'll own it, for better or worse."

For better or worse. Like a marriage. When you get down to it, it is a little like a marriage. Commitment, trust, all that good stuff.

"Anyway," I said, "How's things with your Mom?"

"Mom's fairly stable. I want to believe she'll get better, but I don't think so. So, I build my hopes around her not getting worse, around not being in too much pain."

All I could do is empathize quietly, say a few platitudes. I felt that I was presuming on her too much, given her bigger problem. But she was handling it.

We said our goodbyes, which included a hug.

I couldn't wait to see what was on that flash drive. But I thought better of doing anything with it immediately. I wanted some time to go by since I had met with Sarah, so there would be little chance that it could be associated with her, at least not based on time stamps. But a few days later I put it in right here, on this old laptop that this entire diary is on. I opened the drive and saw numerous folders. I started from the top, and opened the folder labeled "Jim". Well, let's see what Jim's been up to. There were multiple files with innocuous names. 'Vacation', 'Christmas', 'Spring Break' and so forth. Did she give me the wrong flash drive? But I opened "vacation' and saw what I was looking for! Sarah, in her thoroughness, had labeled the files and folders such that they would raise no suspicion if someone saw them.

But the contents were another matter. What Jim did on his 'vacation' was hire his brother-in-law to operate an investigation agency. There was no record of their relationship, and everything looked legitimate. But half of the money that Jim's brother-in-law was paid by CISA ended up in Jim's pocket.

For 'Christmas' Jim got a woman in his office to have an affair with Jim's competitor for a promotion to Head of Investigations. Once the relationship was established, she revealed it, and claimed that she had been coerced into sex. Jim's competitor had to resign and go for Reeducation. Jim got the promotion he wanted, and the woman got promoted to Jim's former position.

And so it went, from one file to the next, with excellent documentation. And there were other folders; Sam, Ophelia, Mary, LeVon, Connie, Taylor and others. I was amazed at what had been going on all this time, and nobody knew. Well, somebody knew. Perhaps lots of people knew. But The People did not know. Yet.

My compatriot came up with his own files. I went through them and was similarly appalled. The part concerning the two Thought Leaders was downright explosive. Some of the cases I was familiar with, but others made me wonder how my compatriot had any knowledge of them. I asked. He said that there were other believers who had their own records. I wasn't sure how to feel about that. This was great information, and there was a wide net, so to speak, wider than I realized. But it also meant that more people were in on this than I realized. How long can a secret be kept among so many people?

And this embarrassment of riches has made me think. If I dumped it all at once, once the transmitters were ready, it would be overkill, more than most people would be prepared to handle. And after that there would be nothing left. I've given it some consideration, and come up with some ideas. I'll dump only a little at a time, and from the lower-level official's cases first. Let it build. Those people who might dismiss the lesser cases as irrelevant would at least be conditioned. And then I'll release more significant information. Not so easy to dismiss.

And I've also been thinking, why not attack from the inside? After all, my accomplices are on the inside. I've contemplated how this could play out. As information becomes public there will be tension in the offices. Fingers will be pointed, as I have experienced previously. Blame will be placed. I can use that. I could get people turned against each other, covering their own butts on the one hand, and playing grievances on the other.

I want a 'grand plan' where I just pull the trigger, and it all happens. But that's unrealistic. I need to play this a little at a time, and make adjustments. With the time I have left until the transmitters are ready, I've mentally played out possibilities, considering various scenarios and how they might work out. If I play this right, aggrieved people within The System might go public, and then there would be no denying the truth. I envision a time, perhaps more of a fantasy than anything, when former members of The System report live from our transmitters on what they know.

125

Entry Twenty-Five

It seems obvious now, but I've had to work my way to the realization; facts don't matter. At least, not much. People believe whatever it is that works for them, and will deny anything that contradicts their belief, even when it is obviously true. And the better 'educated' they are, the more likely people are to entrench themselves in The Truth. I remember reading once, it can be harder to fool a child than an adult. Children have fewer built-in blind spots, developed over time, than adults. But even children learn soon enough to see what is not there, and to not see what is there.

I have my work cut out for me. And I can see that there is an Achilles heel to my plan. I now anticipate rapid developments that will need rapid responses; not just a broad, unresponsive plan. There must be communication out to the transmitters to relay information moment by moment. That pretty much requires transmitters on the inside, and they would be vulnerable. I went to John for thoughts.

We can no longer presume that we are under the radar. We like to think that we are entirely undiscovered, free to associate as we please. But we don't know that. I have to be optimistic, but I have no way of being sure that we haven't been infiltrated. There is at least the possibility that everything I'm doing is being watched. So, John and I meet in varying locations, remote, and easy to spot anyone watching us. I hope.

"For a while," said John, "we could hope that the Thought Police wouldn't even realize we are operating under their nose. But when it hits the fan, when information is circulating that they can't control, you can be sure that the Thought Police will pull out all the stops. What we are doing is unprecedented, so expect the response to be unprecedented. We simply can't be sure what they will do. We'll need to be agile."

He paused for input from me. I had none, so he continued. "Initially they'll look for digital communication. The longer they concentrate on that, the less we would have to worry about them looking for analog transmitters, much less finding them." John paused to contemplate further. "What if we sent the signals digitally, also, as well as analog? The Crawlers would find them quickly enough, and the Thought Police would chase after that, and never even think to look for an analog signal. We could use burner phones, lots of them, and make it look like there's a network operating, that they will try to shut down. But, there will always be new phones and new networks. And no real people to be found, when the Thought Police find the phones. They could rush to the scene of a transmission, but find no one, because no one was ever actually with the phone. My guess is that they would let some of the communications go through, in the hope of tracking down the perpetrators. More wasted time on their part."

Good old John. He's great at seeing a bigger picture. Hell, he *invents* the bigger picture. But I still had concerns. "That sounds like a no-brainer. But it does leave the possibility that they'd catch on too soon. All it takes is one clever guy to wonder about why the cell phone communications never track to an actual person. A clever guy might guess that it's a decoy, and then wonder how the communications are really happening."

John didn't have an immediate answer to that. So, he backtracked to the basics. "We can never be absolutely sure of anything. Risk is part of this. The best thing, I think, is to have multiple transmitters on the inside, but to only use one at a time. Have it broadcast in a short burst, and then move it. Even in this modern age, and presuming the Thought Police finally figured out what it was that they were looking for, it would take at least five or ten minutes for them to track the signal and get to it. By that time, we've abandoned the area and taken the transmitter elsewhere."

John paused just a moment to develop his thoughts. "We should have spotters nearby to remain behind, inconspicuously, to check to see if the Though Police respond. The first time they do, we know that they're on to us, and we could alter our strategy as needed. Also, and I'll have to think about this, but I think we could use a low-power device, such as walkie-talkies to send a signal to be repeated by the transmitter. The advantage is that nobody is at the actual transmitter when it broadcasts, and the walkie-talkie could have such low power, that its signal would not be detected unless a Thought Police scanner was very close. We might mix all these possibilities up, so the Thought Police would never be able determine how it all works."

John would be great at chess. "That sounds like a pretty fair amount of equipment, and a fair number of people. Can you do all this? Can we still be good to go in a week or two? I'm concerned that we might be caught, before we even get started."

"I have people. More than enough. And my people have people. There's more depth than even I know. As for the equipment, that's more of a concern, but we're not looking too bad. On the inside, we aren't having to assemble parts from scratch. As I said before, it's getting parts to the outside, and then constructing them into transmitters that's more of a problem. Not just anybody can do that. I need to send out two of my guys. Correction, *you* need to send out two of my guys."

"I can do that easily enough. But it takes a little time. Do you have your two people ready to get Canceled and get to the outside?"

"Yes, I have them. They can do all that we need, assemble the transmitters and operate them. Of course, they need the parts to assemble.

"You said you have a way to get them the parts."

"Yes, I can make that happen."

"OK. I think it's time to get your guys Cancelled." It seemed so routine to say that. But when I think of the road I traveled to get to this point! John wanted me to Cancel two people, but would not give me the information on who the two people are. He said he wanted it to happen 'organically'. I would get multiple complaints filed from concerned citizens, specifying the Thought Crimes of his two people. I get complaints like that all the time, so how would I know which two were the ones I was looking for? I asked John.

"You'll know. Give yourself some credit."

Chip Kussmaul

Entry Twenty-Six

I don't really need to see Sarah. She has already given me what I need. There is inherent risk in continuing to see her, but I feel the need to. I know myself well enough to know I'm rationalizing; I'm pretending there's a strategic reason to see her. Strange how the mind works. I know why I'm doing this, am consciously aware of it, yet I believe the lies I tell myself. Isn't this like the people who deny the inner compass that tells them to steer away from The System?

Sarah is fifteen years older than me. And that matters, why? We are professionals, engaged now in, dare I say it, the overthrow of The System. What has age got to do with it? Because I'm attracted to her. Because, in normal times, we would probably develop a relationship. That's the way my mind is working now. I'm neck deep in a plot to overthrow The System, but my mind goes first to Sarah and what might be! I am a fool! I am human.

So, I set up another meeting, at a different coffee house, to again interview her concerning the 'he said/she said' incident. It could by rights have been determined a month ago with a finding of 'no further action needed'.

"It's great to see you again," I said. "How have things been going?" Open ended question. I could be referring to anything.

"Things are about the same at work. Those people you were assigned to investigate are getting along, at least for now. They've always had issues with each other. I suspect this truce won't hold."

"I'd best keep the investigation open, just in case."

"Good idea."

"Anything else to report? It's been a little while."

"Well, Mom's still stable. That's not all good. I want her to be better."

There was a look of resignation. It was hard for me to bear, as we both filled the space with a sip of coffee. This was so strange, I thought. We have readily talked of things that, if properly investigated, could lead to our Cancellation. Or perhaps worse, if our plans fell through and The System needed to make an example of us. Yet, talking personally about our feelings for each other was the subject that was difficult to broach. We talked readily of the forbidden, yet were reticent of the permitted.

Then Sarah changed all that. "We've talked about many things, especially about me. But I know little about you. That doesn't seem fair, does it?" She was demure in her asking.

In a strange, satisfying way, I felt defensive. I wanted to dive in all the way. But I didn't want to go too far, all at once. "What's to tell? I'm just a guy who has followed a fairly normal path. I'm pretty much alone, now. My parents were killed in an accident when I was little. I barely remember them. I was raised by my aunt, my father's sister. It was kind of evident that she didn't want to have to. As a child, I kept her from things, I guess. She was never mean or anything, but we never got close. Once I went off to school, we almost never saw each other again." I'd never thought about this too much, until I heard myself saying it.

Sarah reached across the table for my hand. She smiled. "I feel sorry for myself about Mom. But at least I've had her love. I'll always have her love." She turned her eyes down for a moment in reflection, then back up. "I'm losing what some people have never had." She renewed her smile. "Am I the lucky one, or not?"

I smiled back, contemplated her hand on mine. "I think you're the lucky one. I had a bestie. I'm not sure we were ever much more than roommates. We've just recently broken up, and it doesn't mean that much to either of us. So, back at you; am I lucky to not feel the pain? Shouldn't there have been something there for me to lose?"

"Yes, there should have. I know that. I'm losing Mom but then again, I'll always have her." Her smile faded a bit, and then, "I was married. It was a strange thing. Yes, I loved him. And I think he loved me. But love is not enough. Not by itself. We started off great, and I saw a lifetime together. But looking back, I see that I was a bit, well, delusional. There were things that told me there was a problem, but I didn't want to see them. I was happy. I wanted to stay happy. Seeing my husband for what he was, rather than for what I wanted to believe he was, would have been too upsetting. So, I believed the lie." She looked me in the eye, perhaps wondering if she knew for sure who I really was. I hope my eyes told her she could trust me. "He was cheating on me. He was using me. My friends dropped hints, but didn't feel they should confront me. It's funny how sometimes your friends know more about you than you do. But those hints started playing in my mind. And I started taking mental notes. Finally, it all just broke loose in my head. I connected the dots, and they made a picture of a guy who used me, almost for sport. He wanted to see what he could get away with."

She seemed to be able to relate this without too much pain. "How long has it been?" I asked. "I mean, are you divorced now?"

"It's been eight years since the divorce. Eight years, three months, nine days and twenty-seven minutes... Just kidding! Anyway, eight years. You can't go back. What he did to me is a part of who I am forever. But maybe, in a weird way, I'm better for it."

"I don't know what all got you here, but I'm impressed with who you are." That was a bit forthcoming for me, but it felt right to say.

Sarah accepted the flattery graciously. "You take what you've got and make the best of it. I don't pretend anymore, and I'm so much happier with taking the bad with the good, than with pretending it's all good."

"I'll drink to that!" We toasted with our coffee cups.

Chip Kussmaul

Entry Twenty-Seven

I think it's best that I not tell my compatriot about the two 'plants' that John has arranged for me to Cancel. Hell, John hasn't even told me who they are. This movement is growing to the point that I'm not sure who is in, and who is out. The chances of being infiltrated are growing exponentially. So, everyone should only know what they need to know. That includes me and Ted.

Sure enough, the day after I spoke with John about the 'plants' I received anonymous complaints from various people about two radicals who were claimed to be 'disrupting legitimate social interaction'. That's a cookie cutter claim. Lawyers and bureaucrats have simplified the judicial process to the point of a one-size-fits-all 'disrupting social interaction' charge. The advantage in that, right now, is that those claims would not stick out as unusual concerning my two plants.

As I mentioned a while back, it's not that hard to communicate through double-speak, such that the Eavesdroppers don't comprehend what is really being discussed. I didn't know who John's plants would be, but here's the transcript of how one of them told me:

"It says here, Mr. Clark, that you disrupted legitimate social interaction."

"Don't I have a right to a lawyer?"

"You have not been charged, yet. Yes, you can have a lawyer, but that complicates things, and you don't really need one, if you haven't been charged. Sometimes the Court is suspicious of people who demand a lawyer, when they haven't been charged. Do you still want a lawyer?"

"I guess not."

"So, tell me, what is your explanation for disrupting a legitimate social interaction."

"I don't even know what this relates to. I was just apprehended without any explanation. Told that I disrupted a legitimate social interaction."

"But you must know what you did. They didn't bring you in for nothing. The complaints, and there's more than one, weren't filed for no reason. What did you do?"

"Are you telling me to tell you what to charge me with?! That's nuts!"

"I'm giving you the chance to redeem yourself. Chances are, Class One Reeducation is all that's called for, here. But if you don't cooperate, this could move all the way up to Cancellation. You don't want that, do you?"

"I don't want to be treated like a villain, just for what I said."

"Really, and what is it that you said?"

"There were some people praising the security that has been assured to us by the Thought Police and The System. I told them to not be so sure. That's all. I was just shooting off my mouth. I get tired of all the people who just do as they're told, and believe that The System has everything under control. I was just giving them a hard time. Honestly, it's not the first time I've done it. I guess it's just the first time anyone filed a complaint."

"Yes, it is. We have no previous complaints on you. Given the way you're talking to me now, I'm surprised there haven't been previous complaints."

135

"I guess I'm surprised, too. (pause) I've been trying to communicate to people that The System is corrupt. Since you can't get anything out past the Crawlers, I just tell people in person. If I had a way to broadcast it, I would. People should know how corrupt The System really is."

"What makes you think it's corrupt?"

"I just do. Nobody had to tell me, I just know."

"And you refuse to stop doing this?"

"I'd shout it so the whole world could hear, if I had a way."

"OK, now I think you need a lawyer."

"After I've incriminated myself? That's a perfect example of how The System works. Let's just cut out the middleman. Cancel me. I'm glad to go."

The other plant testified in a similar fashion. Now I had my two plants headed to the outside. Each knew to look in the fold in the armrest for final information. We couldn't expect to hear back from them until they had a transmitter up and running.

John already has the receivers up on the inside, waiting for a broadcast. Once we get the signal, it will be time to go for broke. I'm really feeling it. I don't sleep like I used to. I'm typing this at 3 a.m. So many ways for things to go wrong. Have I thought of everything? That's not possible. I can only hope that I have thought of enough. And I know I have some brilliant, dedicated minds working with me.

Our inside transmitters are ready to transmit information to the two people on the outside, who will then rebroadcast to the general public, via the numerous strategically placed receivers on the inside. It seems very convoluted, but this will make it difficult for The Thought Police to track anyone down. And, with luck, it will be weeks before the Thought Police even know to look for an analog signal.

John, bless him, has added some extra security to the system. The inside transmitter will relay messages to the outside receivers via Morse code, as we have discussed. That way, if someone should accidentally pick up the signal, they wouldn't immediately recognize it as subversive. And, to the extent feasible, he is using directional antennas, such that the signal is received only by receivers in line with the antenna. It's not possible to encrypt an analog signal like you can with digital, but so few people know Morse code, it's almost like encryption. Also, John prearranged some 'codes' to the Morse code, words that mean something different to the operators than what they mean to the rest of us. Anything to slow the Thought Police down. For now, the walkie-talkies are not part of this. John is holding them in reserve such that, if/when the Thought Police catch on, he can bring on the walkie-talkies to further confuse them.

I can't know just when that first transmission will come in from the outside. Maybe just days. Perhaps a week or more. When it does, it will be the first communication from the Wilderness to the Inside in decades! It can't happen too soon.

Chip Kussmaul

Entry Twenty-Eight

I so much want to contact Sarah and share all of this with her. But starting now, I have to presume that at least some of us are being watched, watched to see who else we contact. Even under the fairly reasonable pretext under which I've been contacting her, I have to stop. And, in saying that, I recognize that I am the one central link to this effort. I am concerned that, if anything happens to me, this could all collapse. There should be a means of carrying on without me, just in case. I'm considering getting John and my compatriot together so that they can communicate without going through me. But I am a layer of security. If anything broke down, or if either group was infiltrated, it could not bleed into the other group, except through me. And I will have to trust me to not screw it up. I'm feeling the pressure.

I go to work every day like normal. That's the best cover. And I can communicate with my compatriot right under the eyes of the very people we are working against. We just need to be very careful to not arouse any suspicion. For John and me, it's a different story. We have no reasonable cover for why we would ever meet together. And at this point, we don't really need to meet. But I do need to communicate information. So, John will send go-betweens. He will have to find people who, on the one hand, are highly trustworthy but, on the other hand, not closely associated with him. Sometimes I think we're being paranoid, but as they say, just because you're paranoid doesn't mean no one is out to get you!

I've sent a lot of people for Cancellation. I have sent incorrigible thieves. I have sent people guilty of heinous physical assaults. But mostly, I send people who are guilty of misinformation and disinformation. Are these really even crimes? For those who do it inadvertently or innocently, Reeducation will suffice. Those who do it repeatedly and willfully, are Cancelled.

But, what about people who plot to bring down The System? What about people like me? It suddenly occurs to me that maybe not all cases come through my office! Maybe I don't know all the crimes and all the punishments! Could there be an agency, one that we are not told of? One at the highest level whose sole function is to see to people like me? I can believe it's possible. I can't presume it's not. I have presumed so much for so long! We can never be sure of what we don't know. We can only speculate, and that can be dangerous. Yet, speculate we must. The only other choice is to accept what we are told, and I can see how poorly that works for those who seek truth.

Maybe I'm paranoid. Maybe I'm not. I have to consider all possibilities, and I would call that 'rational'. I've come this far, and I won't stop, and I won't waver over concerns of what they might do to us. The phrase keeps coming back to me, "He who hesitates is lost." Interesting. Hesitate about what? We are all supposed to function normally, day to day, accepting the Thought Leader's directives. Hesitate about what? Hesitate concerning taking initiative, thinking for yourself, building your own life, going your own direction. I've read about those things in countless books, but those concepts don't even exist today. Hesitate about what? "He who hesitates is lost." That's a pointless phrase, now, not worth repeating, because almost no one even contemplates initiative in the first place.

The new phrase should be, "Do as you're told." Or "Think what we tell you to think." No, I like that phrase that I read; "He who hesitates is lost." I will not hesitate. I can not. Is The System so well structured that it can stop me? This lethargic, over bureaucratized, self-serving System; can it even keep up with me? I must stay ahead of it, because I know that, if it ever catches up with me, with us, it will consume us, envelop us in its aura of self-serving conformity. Truly, I would rather be dead. If it comes to it, and it might, I would rather be dead. But I will never just lie down and die, I will fight to the end.

Entry Twenty-Nine

The outside transmitters are up! I only know this because John sent a runner over to tell me. Otherwise, I have no way of knowing. The sun still shines, everyone is still going about their business. The insurrection has begun, and no one knows! Perfect. It took the runner a day to 'casually' encounter me and tell me, and then instantly move on. We need quicker communication than that, but at least it works. I previously created numbered flash drives with the pertinent information. John has them. They will be broadcast sequentially. Each has ever increased damning information about higher and higher levels of System corruption. I won't be able to communicate frequently with John, but I can't let this operation run on autopilot, either. Adjustments will need to be made, as we assess how things are going.

I want so much to be with Sarah, to share in this. In fact, I'm feeling very lonely. We should all be together, celebrating this milestone, but instead I just go to work and pretend, along with my compatriot and the others, that everything is normal.

That will change tomorrow. The first broadcast will come back inside the walls. They will send a digital signal, hacked into various established apps. The average person won't be looking for that signal, but they will find them. There's a million apps out there, but when one hits, goes viral, the whole world watches it. I really think that the very nature of what we're transmitting will make it go viral. The more organic this is, the better. It should build from the bottom up, not be force fed, the way the Thought Leaders do.

Crawlers will swat this stuff down as quick as they can. But in doing that, people will begin to wonder about all the things that Crawlers have been keeping from us for all these years. If we can just keep a bit ahead of the Crawlers, bouncing from app to app, enough will get out that people will catch on. If we do this right, the efforts of the Crawlers and of the Thought Police to stop us will make them look bad. And make us look good. I hope. It could go either way, but I've found so many closet believers that I hope for a groundswell.

Entry Thirty

Wow! I wasn't even trying, and our first post appeared in my own feed! It must be in many other people's feeds. It lasted only seconds, and then the Crawlers got it. But if the posts last even a little while, that's enough time. And we will keep posting to various apps. People will see. Some will question why they are not allowed to see.

I went to work this morning. I would have no good reason not to. Also, I was eager to see if anyone had anything to say. I didn't want to be the first one to bring it up, so I just waited. Nothing, at first. But then one of my investigators, Tracy, came to me and told me about what she saw. She told me about a post making seditious claims, and that maybe we should investigate.

"What did it say," I asked.

"I didn't get to read all of it before the Crawlers took it down. But it made claims about some of the clerks in some System departments. I'm sure it's complete disinformation, but that's what we're here to stop."

"Absolutely. But at least the Crawlers got to the post. Quick enough, it appears."

"Well, not quite quick enough. I read a lot of it. And if I did, who knows how many others did?"

"True. OK, well, see what you can uncover about the perpetrator. And if it happens again, take a screen shot, so we can all look at it."

"No problem. It's one thing for the Crawlers to take these posts down, but they should never get up in the first place. Why can't they be stopped ahead of time?"

"Good point," I said. 'But, you know, they've been trying to stop spam texts for as long as anyone can remember; they just keep on coming. You can stop things after the fact, but stopping the bad actors ahead of time without stopping everyone else, is nearly impossible."

"I suppose so. Anyway, I'll catch a screen shot of anything else that comes up."

"Do that. And let me know immediately if it happens. I want to keep on top of it."

"You bet."

She left the office with a positive feeling, appreciative that I had paid heed to her observations. She had no idea yet, what was coming. And through her, I had an inside track on the posts without implicating myself.

Texts!? Besides apps, why not also do random texts, just like the spammers? How do they do that? John was likely to know, or would know people who did. First chance I got, I would suggest it to him, in case it hadn't already occurred to him.

It's hard to appear entirely normal, when things are breaking the way they are! My compatriot and I try to keep the grins off our faces. I thought I should bring up what Tracy, the investigator, had said. It would be normal, expected, for us to do so.

"Tracy was in a little earlier," I said. "She says she got a post giving misinformation about some clerks in some System departments. The Crawlers took it down, of course, but she still got to read some of it.

I told her she should take a screen shot if it happens again, so we can all look at it."

"Yes, a screen shot would help us all see what it's about." It was all he could do to keep the grin off his face.

"It's not our department's responsibility, necessarily, to track the technology that allowed this to happen. But it is our responsibility to investigate the perpetrators. Spreading misinformation is of course a felony and must be stopped."

"No doubt about it," he said with a straight face. "If anything like this continues to happen, we should take charge of locating the perpetrators."

"I think you're right, and I appreciate your initiative. There are other departments that will have an interest, but I think we can reasonably claim to take the lead. I think other departments should report to us, so we have a full dossier of information that would help in any prosecution."

"That makes sense to me. Why would they object?"

"Why, indeed? But let's not jump to conclusions. This is probably just a one-time thing."

"Probably."

It was difficult to get through the rest of the day acting normally. There were the usual cases to investigate and prosecute. It has altered my perspective by a lot, now. I continue investigating infractions of people saying inappropriate things about The System, usually offhandedly and with no real intent. I do that, even as I am working to topple the entire System! If I am ever caught, who would prosecute me? It is cause for concern. There has never been a case such as this. That would mean they would make up the prosecution as they went along. The law, and the punishment, would be whatever they say it is.

Entry Thirty-One

It's been only a few days, and things are developing rapidly. So many things to consider. Sure enough, it had occurred to John to send spam texts, along with the posts, on the social apps. It is now apparent to all that this is more than just a random occurrence. People are reacting. Tracy has her screenshots, of both an app post and a spam text. This stuff is getting out there!

It seemed appropriate to call a staff meeting. Tracy, plus my compatriot, Ted, and the rest of the investigators met in the conference room. I decided to not be a greater presence than I needed to be. I turned things over to Tracy to tell us what she knew.

Tracy seemed eager to take charge.

"I've made hard copies of the screenshots of the spam text and the post I've received. Forwarding them to you by phone might have raised some eyebrows from the people upstairs, so here they are, on paper. What the two things seem to have in common is that they are impugning workers at three of The System's departments. Just one might be some sort of pointless grudge, but three indicates some sort of conspiracy. Before I go any farther, have any of the rest of you received any such posts?"

Out of eight people in the room, six people, including myself, had received posts. Not bad! Two others besides Tracy had managed to take screen shots before the Crawlers took them down.

Tracy continued. "That's a very high percentage. If that is typical of the general population, we have a problem, and it needs solving soon! If you haven't already done so, please save screenshots of everything you get. We'll need to see if we can weave the threads together and find out who is doing this, and why."

Yes, why. We have only been releasing the damning evidence, but have not given a reason why. That seems to be effective. Commonly, some organization, maybe just a kid in the basement, would give an impressive sounding name, 'People for Ethical Government' or some such. But the mystique of having this all come from nowhere and everywhere, and with no organization laying claim, makes the whole thing more mysterious. For a people who like easy answers, having no answers gets their attention. At no time in my memory has the integrity of The System been questioned, except in quiet places among people who trust each other. So far, Tracy is only concerning herself with what is happening, and has not much contemplated the motive of the perpetrators.

Tracy continued. "We have a total of five names given as corrupt officials in these posts. I don't even know if they're real people. We need to find out." Tracy turned to me and asked if it was OK for her to assign investigators to check out the stories.

I quickly weighed the possibilities. If she took charge, I wouldn't be able to manipulate the investigations. But I wanted to diversify the reach of the investigation, to dig as deep and relentlessly as possible. I felt that Tracy would be that relentless person. She would keep digging, and that's what I wanted. I gave her the go ahead.

Tracy assigned an investigator to each of the posts. They would speak directly with the people mentioned. I said that, where possible, they should meet in person, at that person's office. That would get feet in the door of various departments and agencies. Who knows what else might turn up when they did that.

So far, it hadn't occurred to Tracy to try to find the digital source of the posts. Not surprising. Our department is centered around investigations of people and motives. The technical aspects went to other departments. Sooner or later, it would occur to her to trace the sources digitally but, right now, she was presuming that interviewing the parties mentioned would yield the needed information.

Entry Thirty-Two

It's been a great few days! So far, I have heard no mention of these posts from folks I encounter. I know that many, even most, have been receiving them. I think there's two things keeping people from talking. First, spam is common enough that people tend to pay little attention. Second, the posts run counter to the presumption that The System is irreproachable. Therefore, people presume that the posts are lies, and that to discuss them constitute spreading of disinformation. Discussing them could get people in trouble, and so they just keep quiet. Thanks to Tracy and, I'm sure, others, the validity of the posts will be discovered. I'm confident that the posts will become a hot topic before long.

But not online. Any discussion of this online would be taken down by the Crawlers in moments. And if a person gets too many demerits for 'misinformation' posts, they get Censored from the internet for a period of time. It's irrelevant whether the information is accurate or not.

Nobody discusses this online, and that's good. I want people to begin to feel the extent to which they are being manipulated. After lifetimes of staying within bounds like good little citizens, I want them to start feeling resentment. They will discuss these posts in private, and start to wonder how clean The System is; to what extent The System is there for them. To what extent they have been manipulated their entire lives. Some, I know, will be fine with all of it. They want the security. They are willing to pay the price in personal integrity and in basic freedom. But others. Others will rebel. How many are there like that? We are about to find out.

Entry Thirty-Three

It's been a week since my previous entry. This whole thing is blowing up! Just as I hoped, people are discussing the posts somewhat openly. Every day John is sending new posts concerning low level corruption in various agencies. I think this will leave the higher ups a little confused. If they go public, they are acknowledging the rot. If they try to cover it up, it might look even worse. Either way, I win.

People are saving screenshots. Those being named in the posts are not the isolated high-level executives but the everyday office workers. People know the people who are being revealed. They know the claims are true. For The System to label it 'disinformation' would damage their facade of integrity. I predict that the executives will make examples of the people named in the posts, make examples of them and promise to clean house of the corruption. In doing that, they acknowledge the corruption. And then, we release the information we have on the higher-ups. They will have set themselves up. There will be investigations during that house-cleaning. And what department will handle that? MY department!

Earlier today, I was walking out of Starbucks with a coffee. Another man who had been standing by the door with a coffee of his own, bumped into me as we were both leaving. He spilled some of his coffee on me and apologized profusely. He had a napkin and was wiping off my shirt. I told him not to worry about it, I would take care of it myself. He insisted. As he wiped my shirt, he said, in the same tone in which he had apologized, but more quietly, "Be at the Starbucks on Fifth, tomorrow at 10:00 am. Sit in the back." And he walked off. To all appearances this was an innocent encounter among strangers.

I was there a little early. I got my coffee and opened my laptop as so many others do. I made myself not look around. I wanted to be as inconspicuous and unmemorable as possible, which means no interaction, even by sight, with others. After a while, a woman came to my table and acted like she knew me. She sat down with little fanfare, so as not to be conspicuous.

"It's been a while. Good to see you again," she said.

"Good to see you, too."

"How are things going at the office?"

I wasn't sure if this was banter, or a real question. I played it both ways. "Largely it's just the usual. But we're finding a number of unusual posts concerning alleged corruption at System offices. I doubt that much, if any, of it is true. But of course, we have to investigate. I've got a team on it doing in person interviews with the people who have been named. My people are good. Whatever there is to find, they're likely to find it. I don't want to overplay my hand, but I'm planning on getting my department named lead investigative agency for these posts. I think they are going to be a major issue, requiring full cooperation and integration among all departments and agencies. Someone has to take charge of that. It might as well be me."

"Interesting. People have been talking about the posts. They're making a stir. But do you think you are in a position to head up such a committee?"

"If I time it right. The posts have to be enough of a bother that the entire System is concerned, but not big enough that the big wigs will want to get personally involved. If I time it right, they'll just about give it to me."

"Well, that would be a great career move!"

"I suppose so. But I have to time it right. I wouldn't want any info on the higher-ups being released before I get the committee established."

"Of course, not."

"And if there became a critical mass of exposure of lower levels of corruption, such that it had to be acknowledged by The System, then if higher level corruption was uncovered after that, there would be no way to keep it covered up. No way to keep it censored."

"I can see your point. I think anyone would agree with you."

"Apparently, from books I've read, something very much like this happened earlier in the twenty first century. There was a feeding frenzy on upper-level officials."

The woman nodded at that observation. We both took a sip of coffee, and then she made her own observation. "Speaking of how things were back in time, I've become aware of something they called Xerox machines. The older ones were like a printer, but were not digital. They could make copies very efficiently, as efficiently as anything today. But you had to start with a real copy to duplicate, not a digital file. I've heard there are some of these machines still around, and people who know how to make them work. Imagine if tens of thousands of leaflets went out, with no way for Crawlers or Thought Police to trace a source. Do you think that would be a problem, relative to your investigation?"

Brilliant! "Yes, I know of these machines, and yes, if they were used to disseminate the information we are investigating, it would be far more difficult to track anything back to the perpetrators. Let's hope they don't think of that, right?"

"Right."

153

I contemplated a moment. "And what if these people had contact with the Canceled people in the Wilderness, and the Canceled people told everyone they didn't mind being Canceled at all. Especially if they used their real names, and photos, and people recognized them? If that got distributed in Xeroxes, it could be very damaging; really make people question what they've been told their whole lives."

She only nodded, and I went on, "I need to be able to think like the perpetrators, in order to better find them. I think they would do that, use Xeroxes. Why wouldn't they? One of the most effective points to Cancellation is that people think it's almost a fate worse than death. If it proved to not be like that, there might be a line for Cancellations! But that's all speculation. I've recommended Cancellation for countless numbers of people, and I don't even know what it consists of. But you know how rumors are."

"Of course. I was just speculating about the Xeroxes and such. Just another one of those rumors. I suppose we shouldn't repeat speculation and rumors."

"Well, as an investigator and prosecutor, a certain amount of speculation is called for. But we can't jump to conclusions. We can't rush in without considering consequences."

 "I couldn't agree more. I think my friends would all agree with you on what you say."

"And I with them. Give them my best."

"I will."

Entry Thirty-Four

I knew from the beginning that CISA, within the DHS, would be the first to jump into investigating the source of the posts. It's their job, after all. As of right now, I don't know how effective they're being at their job. Not fully effective, clearly, because the posts are still coming in regularly. I don't know how John is getting the signals through or how they get into the network, and apparently neither does CISA. Things are moving too fast for me to be able to count on Sarah getting back to me. Besides, communicating with her is a risk, and she doesn't have access to all the information anyway.

I want to have an inside track on this, and I think now is the time to suggest the creation of the task force, headed up by me, of course. It is recognized System wide that the posts are a chronic problem. The finger-pointing has begun, and this is a good time to step in. Staff throughout the System are anxious and upset. After all, the people in these agencies are some of the most emotionally and intellectually reticent people in our city. They take these jobs because they are fully secure and entail little personal responsibility. They do not take stress well, and when something upsets their routine, they are eager to turn to a 'leader' who will ease their minds.

That's where I come in. I went to Lorna with some information, most of it true, about the extent and reach of the posts. I told her we'd found some links that might lead us to the perpetrators. But we couldn't do it all ourselves, we would need information and cooperation from other agencies. I reminded her of how effective my campaign to uncover seditionists had been. Hundreds had been culled from the population who had been preaching their anti-Systemic rhetoric.

They had all been, or were scheduled to be, Cancelled. Without the efforts of my team, they might all still be out there.

I made my case effectively, and Lorna agreed to get together with the relevant department heads to consider forming a task force. It took less time than I thought it would, but still it was nearly two weeks before she got back to me, called me into her office.

"You've got a green light on this. In fact, they want you moving as quickly and efficiently as possible on this. I had easy buy-in from everyone but CISA. Not surprisingly, they aren't eager to share their information. They've always been tight with their data, but they are required to give you full cooperation. If it doesn't turn out that way, let me know, and I'll apply some pressure."

"Thanks, Lorna. I see no way for the perpetrators to hide, when we have our own boots on the ground plus the online data from CISA. We'll find them, I promise."

"The sooner the better. I'm feeling the heat from above. This isn't even supposed to be possible in the first place, and the longer it goes on, the more we're all going to feel the effects."

"I couldn't agree more. I'll keep working on the case, you can be sure."

When the conversation was over, I stood up to leave, and Lorna came from behind her desk, shook my hand, and thanked me. That was a bit odd. We've worked together for years and formalities such as this weren't generally practiced. She really was feeling the heat, and she really was counting on me.

I went straight back to my own office and called in my compatriot.

"We've got the green light. Now we have to get this organized, ASAP. I don't want CISA, or anyone else setting their own strategies ahead of us. We need to try to get them used to answering to us, and not the other way around."

"CISA's department head is a tough case," Ted pointed out. "Most people in The System just want predictable jobs. Some want to advance in their careers, but even they still want an easy, predictable path. That's why they're in The System. Ken Stillers is a different case. He's dedicated. I don't imagine he'd be easy to fool, if someone wanted to fool him."

"Yes, I know that's all true. It's good to see such dedication at CISA, but we still have a right to expect Stillers' cooperation with this task force. Butting heads with him is a losing proposition. We need a way to get his cooperation, even at a minimum level. I don't know of anyone else who would stand in the way of what we are doing. We need a way, either around him, or through him, to see what they've got. And time is of the essence."

"But you head up the task force. You can insist on compliance."

"Anybody can insist on anything they want. The issue is, what will they get? Ken is no fool, and he is a hard head. If I take him head-on, he'll cause trouble that I don't need. And he'd slow things down, which I also don't need. Let me think about it, and I'll see what I can come up with."

I called the other investigators in to tell them of the task force. We celebrated for a bit, and then I sent them out, telling them to keep digging. They ~~had~~have greater authority now, as members of our new Anti-subversion Task Force (ATF). They would be stirring up discontent and apprehension in multiple departments of The System.

And I have been thinking about Ken Stillers. I've never liked him, but I somewhat respect him. He sets his own agenda, makes up his own mind. Isn't that what I wish everyone would do? But he has no sense of fairness. He will do whatever it takes, hurt whoever gets in his way or fails to comply. Now, *that's* a problem.

I have dirt on him, just as I do with a lot of people in the System. What can I do with it? I want to hold off on the reveals of the people at the higher levels of The System, until things have had a good chance to percolate. But I might have to make an exception for Ken. But how? If I send the information out, he will have to resign. But that would take a while, and it might have an undesired effect. The department heads might circle the wagons around him. I want to hit all of them all at once, so they are each too busy with their own problems to form a useful coalition.

I see no easy answer. What if the dirty information I have was texted directly to Ken? That would put him on the defense, but that might just make him more dangerous. The old saying is, if you encounter a bear, either avoid it, or kill it. Whatever you do, don't wound it. I see no way to take Ken down. He will be a presence through this, as near as I can tell. I want to hold him off to the side, but I can't avoid him entirely.

Entry Thirty-Five

The Xerox idea is brilliant! Copies have been showing up just anywhere, and they can't be tracked back to anyone or anything. It's interesting, when you see how effortlessly the Crawlers take down digital content; this content on paper is always there. Thought Police are going around, almost like litter collectors, trying to round up individual Xerox copies. It's hopeless. They were never prepared for this, and they have no idea how to handle it!

Copies are everywhere, and they vary in content. It's almost like the baseball cards that some people still collect. People collect various of the Xeroxes, and for all I know they trade them like they do ~~the baseball~~baseball cards. There's never been a law against owning a Xerox copy, so the Thought Police aren't even sure what they can enforce. But it took no time for the Thought Leaders to proclaim that the Xeroxes are subversive, and people in possession of them can be prosecuted for sedition. But the interesting thing is, there are so many of them, and so many people collect them, that if any serious effort was made to arrest people, I think all hell would break loose. This is what I've been hoping for! The Citizens are asserting their will on their own, in direct defiance of The System and the Thought Police. Really, they are defying the Thought Leaders, which has never happened before!

The Xeroxes have various content, but many of them profile Cancelled people. They have been hugely effective. They include photos of the Cancelled people, with their families if they have one. These Cancelled individuals tell of why they were Cancelled. They talk of how they were repressed simply for having thoughts of their own instead of following the dictates of the Thought Leaders. And they talk of their life in Cancellation. It's not an easy life. They have to keep at work to raise crops and keep livestock. They have to build their own houses. Houses! Yes, they have houses of their own, rather than the tiny apartments that we have. They have views of nice scenery, uninhibited by a big wall. They can go anywhere. "I could walk around the ~~world~~world, and no one would try to stop me," said one of the Cancelled. He'd have to do some swimming as well, but the sentiment is true. Citizens haven't considered such things in many decades. The young have never experienced it at all.

It's kind of strange, this awakening from acquiescence. People have for so long been so willing to go along. I don't suppose people generally believed that the Thought Leaders were really the smartest, wisest ones. It was just easier to go along. It's like a belief system, I think. A person can have a religion, eat certain foods, wear specific clothing, practice rituals. Why? There is comfort in that conformity. A sense of belonging and security that something greater than yourself is watching over you. So many questions are answered for you, saving the trouble and the angst of seeking your own truth. The answers are so ingrained that people forget what the questions are.

Yes, there is a human need for some of that. A lot of that, in the case of some people. I've read a lot about religions and cultures in the books. They were far more diverse than they are today. I still don't know what to make of it. Some religions, and their practices, seem harmless enough. Nobody got hurt. They seem to help hold families and communities together.

But sometimes religions were behind wars and persecution. It's a confused mess that I have yet to sort out and make sense of. But I do think that it largely comes down to the leaders. Different leaders had different visions, and people went along. And perhaps that's the problem. Why go along? And if a person goes along, it should be a rational decision based on consideration of the realities, not based on faithfully believing whatever their leaders tell them.

That's the problem. That's why I'm doing what I'm doing. The Thought Leaders have been an official government agency for about fifty years, now, although we are led to believe that they have been an omnipresence since the beginning of mankind. We are led to believe that their wisdom has been handed down to them over centuries, millennia, of great human thought, and that they therefore are not to be questioned or challenged. But my books tell me different. There has been turmoil, ebb and flow, good and bad for man's entire existence. When I think about it, I'm not sure we've gotten anywhere. We have greater comfort. Science and technology have worked wonders. But are people wiser? Can they see greater distances and better comprehend themselves? It doesn't appear that way. If anything, it is the opposite. So many people have been so willing to go along, and NOT think, NOT ponder, NOT weigh the possibilities. So many people just want to be given answers, and to hell with the questions.

But that is changing. Something has been pent up, that no one knew was there. If people were truly happy, within themselves, the efforts of my compatriots and I would fall flat. But here we are, on the cusp of….What?

Chip Kussmaul

Entry Thirty-Six

It's been a few weeks. It has become hopeless for the Thought Police to try to reign in the Xeroxes. People carry them, discuss them, with little concern for being overheard or Eavesdropped. This is more than I could have hoped for, but we have to move on from here. If it stays like this, it might fade.

I really want to sit and talk with John. His insights mean a lot to me. He knows things that I don't, and perhaps vice versa. Is it safe to meet with him? I'm not sure. I'll leave it in his hands.

I went to the Starbucks where the woman met with me. I can tell that John's people are always watching me, and I figured that if I went there at ten a.m. as before, that would signal them that I wanted to meet. Five minutes after I sat down, a middle-aged man came and sat with me, talking as if we'd always known each other.

"Hey, great to see you again," he said. "It's been a while. Fill me in on the latest."

"Good to see you, too." We sipped our coffee. "Well, as for the latest, I've certainly been busy. We're still trying to find who is behind all these posts, and the Xeroxes. We don't know what organization is doing this, but my investigator tells me that CISA has determined that the breech is coming from outside the authorized servers. They say it's coming in from wi-fi, not through cable. And apparently the signal keeps moving. They know the signal they are looking for, but every time they get a bead on it, by the time they get to the location, it's gone. Then it comes from somewhere else. CISA said in a report that, if the signal lasted for more than a minute, they'd have a chance of triangulating and getting an exact location. But the signals never last that long. They last just seconds, and you can transmit a lot of data, even in a few seconds."

"That's interesting. You'd think CISA would be technologically capable of just about anything."

"You'd think. They may have to depend on luck. They're setting up triangulation locations in a number of locations, more every day. Their hope is to be able to catch a signal in a zone that they are already covering. They figure that, with the signal constantly moving, sooner or later it's going to be in one of the zones they're covering, and then they'll know the precise location."

"That's ingenious. But if the signal moves, could they get to the physical location quickly enough to catch anyone?"

"Good question. CISA has speculated about that, too. They say that if the signal is within the walls, it's only a matter of time. But if it's outside the walls, it's a whole new problem. They are putting together a task force to go out and patrol. They would have some possibility of finding them, but the area is so vast, the odds are not good."

"Yes, I would think so."

"One thing I forgot to ask them is, are they looking only for digital signals? I don't know if they are making any effort to track analog because, after all, nobody uses it anymore. I didn't want to bring it up. They might wonder why a guy with my limited expertise would ever wonder about an analog signal. So, I have said nothing. And I have heard nothing from anyone else about analog."

"So analog signals within the walls might never even have been noticed?"

"As far as I can tell, that's true. Nothing in the reports or in conversations indicates that scanning analog is within their protocol."

163

"Well, as you say, why would they. Nobody uses analog anymore."

"True enough."

"Well," he asked, "What else is going on in your life? It can't be all office, all the time, right?"

"Funny you should ask. I have a dear friend who I haven't seen in months. I'd love to sit down and talk. You can't say everything in an email. I've been thinking about getting together and catch each other up."

"That would be great, I'm sure. But with everything that goes on in life, sometimes getting together just isn't possible."

"Yeah, I know. I'm thinking I'll leave it to him. If he can, and if he wants to, he'll reach out to me, I'm sure. But it would be good to catch up. Discuss our plans for the future; that sort of thing."

"Sure, it would." He looked at his watch. "Well, I have someone I need to see, so I should be going. It's been great talking. Best of luck in the future!"

"Same to you."

I guess I'm just human. Since that meeting, I'm very anxious to see John. To some extent, I feel like I'm faking it. Yes, I've taken initiative and made important decisions, and they've worked. So far. I've found the people I need, and they've found me. But can I say I have a plan? Yes, sort of. But I'd be deluding myself if I pretended that I can foresee the future. I have ideas more than I have plans. I need help with the plans.

Entry Thirty-Seven

It's been a little surreal. Here I am, leading one of the biggest investigations in anyone's memory. And I'm the one they're looking for! I feel almost like that guy, that guy they're looking for, is someone else. Is it really me? I lead the investigation like I would any other, everything by the book. At the same time, I see how pointless it is. I've sent the investigators to interview the various clerks and their superiors concerning the alleged misdeeds among them. You name it, it's been alleged. For some, it's nepotism, a small enough crime, really, especially when kept quiet. But when it's common knowledge, it's a problem that needs solving. Same for kickbacks. And for the usual sexual misdeeds. The veneer is unraveling, revealing ugliness that The System cannot endure.

I think it's the failure to maintain the façade. That's what upsets so many people. It's not that The System has let corruption happen, but that they've failed to keep a proper appearance, a veneer of propriety. Sort of like the wife who doesn't mind so much that her husband cheats, but she'll go ballistic if he is seen in public with his honey. Keep it quiet, pretend it's a secret, and that's enough for some people.

And that is what has The System in trouble. My investigators go to various offices, people dread seeing them coming now, and it's that it is all in the open that is so upsetting to them. They see their names, their friends' names, and their family names in the posts, and it's not an embarrassment of guilt, it's an embarrassment of having been caught. In interviews, as the guilty parties point fingers at each other, it's not to blame the other for the crime, but for leaving the loose ends that got them caught. I have to say, I didn't think it would be like this. But it's working out, all the same.

Many offices are now essentially nonfunctional. Too many workers are at each other's throats, undermining each other, for any work to be done. Perhaps it's telling that this all makes little difference. Everything outside The System just keeps humming along. I think the general public is also recognizing that, and wondering…

But, what now? Is it time to release the information on the top officials? I've been saving the best for last; the information I have on the Thought Leaders. I think it's best to let them stew. They have to be wondering what anyone knows about their own misdeeds, and I think they might trip themselves up without my help. We'll see.

All of this pondering is just to help me get my head straight, because I expect to be meeting with John soon, and I want to be concise and on point. If/when we collapse The System, then what? Honestly, my one goal has been freedom. My goal has been to defend my right to my own autonomy and individuality. Still, somebody has to run things. Who? And how well will they do?

Entry Thirty-Eight

Leave it to John. I had been told by one of his intermediaries, who appeared out of nowhere as usual, that John would meet with me. She had casually approached me on the sidewalk, walking her dog, who was eager for me to pet him. So, I did. This all seemed to me to be a classic pick-up situation. Smiles and banter, and all that. But within that conversation she revealed that she was an intermediary for John. After several minutes, she told me she had to go, but that I should continue in the direction I had been going and turn left into the building with the red awning. I causally wished her well and said a goodbye to the dog, and headed as casually as I could pretend to the red awning.

It was an older commercial building with signs that said it was a law office. I opened the door and entered into an enclosed vestibule, with a second door. I tried the second door, but it was locked. I wondered what to do for a moment, but then it was opened, and I recognized the guy from Starbucks. He welcomed me warmly into the main lobby area and then sent me through another door at the back.

John welcomed me in, and we shook hands. The room was a little sparse, but it had what you would expect from a law office. There was a large but basic desk in the middle and an array of bookcases with a multitude of books. The desk had a chair to go with it, but John led us to two chairs against a side wall.

"It's good to see you," John said. "You're looking well."

"I can say the same for you. I was beginning to wonder if I'd see you again."

"We can't do this too often and we must pay attention to what's going on around us. But I don't think it's realistic to do everything with go-betweens. So, let's talk."

I wonder if there's anything that could get John agitated. Here we were, trying to take down The System, and apparently succeeding, and he was no more concerned than if he was ordering lunch. I gathered my thoughts for a moment. "We have a lot to discuss concerning strategy, going forward. But, speaking of forward, I'm not sure, at this point, what that really is. If we take down the System, are we done? What happens next?"

John smiled affably. "We're never done. If people had kept at it all along, we wouldn't be facing what we are right now. So, we do all that we can to gain freedom and a workable government, and then we work to keep it that way. Oh, and we destroy the Wall so that people are free to come and go as they please."

The Wall. "Not so long ago," I said, "I would have cautioned about all the bad people, the aggressive foreign interests who would love to get inside the Wall and take over. Now it appears to not be so true. Still, I'm too informed to not know there are real dangers out there. In spite of everything, The System and the Thought Police do protect us."

"From what?... And, who protects us from them?"

My turn to smile. "That's why I'm here. It's almost scary how successful we're being. We are led to believe that The System is invincible, but it's nothing like that. It can be toppled any time enough people want to take it down. Is that a fault of The System, or of The People? Is every government like that? Do we need something stronger?"

"First, what do you mean by 'strong'? There's more to strength than just physical strength. And that's what we're examining right now.

We are mentally stronger than The System. They've been unchallenged for so long, they don't have it in them to assert control. The strength we have, the resolve, is hard to beat."

"Sure, I get your point. But the strength we have can't stop a bullet. I know nobody's even seen a bullet in decades. But I know that somebody has them, and it's not us." I caught myself. "It's *not* us, right?"

John looked me in the face while he contemplated his answer. That was a bad sign. A simple 'no' would have sufficed. No such luck. "I think you're beginning to see the obvious," he said. "Freedom is an ideal, not a true physical reality. Proclaiming freedom is fine, when everyone is willing to go along with you. But proclaiming your freedom only really counts for something when you are prepared to assert that freedom. That sometimes involves speeches, or ballots. And sometimes it involves physical force. It's reality. Those who refuse to fight are tacitly agreeing to be a slave."

Not what I wanted to hear. "But it's working. What we're doing. We're bringing down The System without any physical violence."

"Good, so far," John said. "And maybe it will all work out. But we are creating a power vacuum. Nobody out there in the Wilderness and beyond owes us any favors. Whatever they want from us, if they have the guns and are willing to use them, either we fight back, or just give up our freedom all over again. There's other cities. They know what's happening here. Who knows how they intend to deal with it?"

"Honestly, I haven't thought that large, or that far ahead. But it's clear that you have. So, you tell me. It's why I'm here. What do we do next?"

"You know the story of the fall of totalitarianism back in the 20th century. In some ways it worked out. In others, well, it didn't. Many people died. But we seemed to be going in the right direction. Then, right in front of everyone, the totalitarians retook control, and we ended up with The System. It's more pervasive than just this city. Yes, The Systems vary; they're different in other cities. But then again, they're essentially the same."

I cut in, partly because I didn't want to hear what he might say next. "I just want for us to be free. We can't expect to free the entire world." I wish I could have left it there, but I knew there was more to consider. "You're saying that we'll need to carry this beyond the Wall, aren't you?"

"Either we push against them, or they push against us. Or both. There's never going to be some happy time when we all get along. It's never happened. It' never going to."

"Why the hell not?! I don't get how so many people can want to just have a nice life, their own way, yet we aren't enough to stop the totalitarians."

John considered me. We were equals, but now he seemed to doubt my competence, my comprehension. "One farmer with one sheep dog can control countless sheep. Look at the citizens right now. They're enjoying watching the System collapse. They're loving the sense of freedom, being able to criticize The System openly. But it has cost them nothing, so far. If things go to hell, how hard will they fight? What are they willing to sacrifice?...How hard will *you* fight? What will *you* sacrifice?"

All that I had put into this, and John dared to question me? I couldn't reject his words; I respected him too much. "The way you're talking, I'd have been better off doing nothing."

"Doing nothing would be easier. A whole lot less stress. Freedom is not stress free. But *you* came to *me*. Remember? You wanted to find out about walkie-talkies, way back when. You weren't even sure why, but you sensed that communication was the key. You craved a way to communicate with others without The System listening in. You wanted to be able to express your own mind. You went to quite a lot of trouble, only so that you could learn to assert your freedom. Be your own man." He had me thinking. "Are you willing to die trying?"

That hit me with a jolt. I remember saying that I was willing to die. Oddly, I could face death more readily than I could face a lifetime of fighting for my freedom. If freedom is so much work, is it worth it? But as John said, look what I've gone through to get here. And I can't go back. I know I can't. I tried to phrase those thoughts in my answer. "I was hoping for some end point. I was anticipating some point where we've succeeded, and we get to live happily ever after. It's sobering to realize that we'll never see that day." I looked to him for a response, but he offered none. "But OK, what now? I think it's close to time to turn loose all the information, all the way to the top levels of The System. I hesitate, because I realize that's all I've got. That's it. Whatever happens after that, I don't know what I can do about it."

"What comes after that is we get people focused on tearing down the Wall. We try to get citizens used to being responsible for their own lives. We stop taking apart what exists, and try to replace it with something better. It's a different mindset, one that some revolutionaries never get the hang of. They're great at the destruction part, but suck at the rebuilding."

I saw his point. If my efforts were to mean anything, I would have to try to guide people from celebrating their independence from The System and into a sense of personal responsibility. How well would that go? It occurred to me that very little of anything like that had been done lately. People live and breathe bureaucracy and programs, and various government departments. It has gotten to be a way of life, unfortunately. Maybe there is not the distinction to be made that I thought there was. Maybe too many people want The System, that it is a symbiotic relationship. Yes, sheep have need of the farmer and his sheep dog. The farmer and his dog bring them to the pastures, and protect them. How would the sheep function without the farmer and his dog?

But then I thought of those Cancelled people in the Wilderness. They could handle it. They *were* handling it. And they like it that way. Would they be willing to come back into the city to straighten things out? Would the people in the city want them here? Just when I thought I was getting to the end, I find that I am really just beginning. Every answer leads to more questions. I had one more question for John. "You never said if you have the bullets."

"No, I didn't"

Entry Thirty-Nine

Before I left the 'law' office, John fixed me up with a communication device, a modern walkie-talkie. It's capable of talking back and forth, but that's not how he wanted me to use it. It has low power, with a range of a few hundred yards. John said that he's always had people close by me, I just didn't know it. Actually, I sort of did know. John told me that there was someone always within range of me, with a walkie-talkie. Also, my new walkie-talkie had been programmed to switch channels at specific intervals, as has also been done with his team's walkie-talkies. They were analog, so Crawlers couldn't detect them, but anyone else who happened to have a receiver could potentially hear. So, he said, use it only sparingly, and for very short periods of time, and presume others are listening. And although his team was always listening, don't expect them to reply. While receiving, they are undetectable, but when transmitting, detectable. Even with all those limitations, I felt better, less isolated.

Isolation is becoming a real thing, anyway. Every day I go into the office, living a lie. Heading up an investigation that is looking for me. My compatriot knows, but we can't say much directly. It's a funny, lonely feeling, with so much on my mind, so many people around, yet no one to communicate it to.

Tracy, my lead investigator, came into my office today. She had some concerns and wanted to discuss them.

"Morale is down. By a lot'" she said. "We are largely investigating our own people, some of whom we know personally. At first, we thought we were just after some bad apples that needed to be culled out. But there's so many of them that I don't know what will be left after we clean house. People are turning on each other. Some are even coming to us instead of us coming to them. They want to air dirty laundry, settle grudges against co-workers. I don't get it. These people have worked together for years, but now it's like the civil war of cubicles."

I should have been delighted. It's what I planned on. But it was getting so ugly. "What we've had, all these years, was dirty. It looked clean, but it was dirty. We have to clean it up for real, so it's not just pretense… Tracy, you know I'm willing to listen, if only so that you can unburden yourself; or if you have any thoughts or ideas, you know I'm always ready to listen."

Tracy organized her thoughts. She focused on a spot on the wall, and then turned back to me. "I'm not sure why we're doing this. I mean, we're catching people red-handed in all kinds of things, and that's our job. But morale is in the toilet, even the other investigators. Their hearts aren't in it anymore. And I've been thinking about something; this all hasn't happened without the upper brass knowing about it. It couldn't have. I think what we're finding at the lower levels is because it's been tolerated, maybe even encouraged at the upper levels. We nail the people at the lower levels. And some of them rat out the people around them, but we haven't gotten to the top. There's no way they're clean at the top. If you want to get rid of bad apples, I think we should be going to the top."

Tracy impressed me with that. She was seeing more than was immediately visible to her. But I had another concern. "I have to ask; what about our department? Have you found anything?"

"Well, yes," she said. "There's a little smoke, but no fire. I have to admit I haven't spent as much time in our department as I should, because I'm afraid of what I might find. To be honest, maybe there should be an independent investigation of our department, to avoid any bias, or even appearance of bias."

"You make a good point. I'll look into making that happen." But what of Tracy's instincts about the top brass? Tracy wasn't yet aware of what I had on the upper brass. She would know before too long. But what power would we be able to exert over them, even after they were exposed? "But, as for your concerns about the top floors, I don't know how we do that. Realistically, I can't send you into the top floors and have you interrogate people who can swat us down like flies."

"I know you can't. But that's where the problem is, I'm sure of it."

"Is this just you talking? Are the other investigators on board with you?"

"We talk some. Most agree that there's trouble at the top, but they don't necessarily want to go there. But when it comes to off the record conversation, Jim agrees with me. If we don't go to the top, then why are we doing any of this? But the other investigators just want to do their jobs and then go home at night."

Where to go from here? I had Tracy eager to do all the damage she could, just the way I wanted. But to what end? She was asking me for permission, or at least for a way, to get to the top. Even with all that I had at hand, I wasn't sure how to do it. I would release the damning information concerning the top brass, just as I had for the others. But was there any way to get to them? Even if the whole city knew the whole truth, well then what? Would the division heads all quit in disgrace? Not a chance.

I said to Tracy, "You've hit me with a conundrum. We see the problem, but don't see a solution. I'm going to have to consider. In the meantime, if you come up with any more thoughts, let me know immediately."

"OK, and one more thing…"

"What?"

"You should know that the one division head who seems cooperative is Ken Stillers at CISA. Anything we ask for, we get. We're working both ways to get to the perpetrators of these leaks. He's doing it from the technology side, we're doing it from the personnel side. He's certain that the leaks are coming from inside The System, because who else would know these things? We're trying to triangulate on who would have, or what group would have, the knowledge that they're disseminating. It's kind of a process of elimination. We eliminate who it can't be, and whoever is left, that's who it is."

"OK, that makes sense." My heart was pounding.

"And Ken and I talked about my reluctance to investigate our own department. He said that if we want an independent investigator, he has a recommendation. You should call Ken."

"I'll do that. Thanks."

Tracy got up and left, and I sat and thought. Great. Tracy and Ken are on a first name basis. I need some way to go from here, and I don't know what it is. I cannot have Ken involved in investigating my department, but Tracy is too sharp to not notice if I stonewall. I have to wonder what Ken has on his mind. What, if anything, does he suspect?

Entry Forty

Well, it's hitting the fan, all right!   John has been releasing information on the higher ups, and now it's panic time in The System. Previously we had been hearing the speeches from the higher-ups about how terrible it was that corruption had found its way into The System, the very system that had been created to thwart greed and corruption. The Thought Leaders and System Administrators had assured us that they would 'get to the bottom of this' and clean things up.

But now, the System Administrators have been shown to be corrupt. It's worked according to my plan. By starting at the lower levels, the higher ups didn't react quite so defensively. For a fatal moment, they didn't know how to handle the leaks. Not so much 'handle', since they couldn't stop them, but how to spin them so that they did the least damage. With people talking among themselves, and with most of the leaks having been verified (thanks to my department), the Administrators had little choice but to acknowledge the corruption and promise to clean house. And then we released the dirt on the higher-ups.

That was one hell of a chess move on my part. I got the Administrators themselves to acknowledge the massive corruption. And then I sprung the leaks about the Administrators' own corruption at the top. Where could they go from there? I had them cornered, sort of.

But they have the power. Almost overnight, after the release of dirt on the higher-ups, the Thought Police started cracking down on any communication concerning the leaks. They have arrested almost a thousand people for possession of subversive material, the xeroxes. And, of course, those who most vociferously objected to having their xeroxes taken were the first to be arrested. I know, because it's on me to prosecute them. What's worse, The System Administrators are meeting to determine if the current form of Cancellation needs to be 'enhanced'.

The timbre in the city has changed. The feeling of celebration has been replaced with a sense of repression. In a sense, we are no more repressed than we ever were, but now people have become more sensitive to it. They had a taste of freedom and independence, and now they're seeing it snatched back away from them.

I am worried. Very worried. So much has gone right, but maybe not enough. The System has had decades to develop, entrench itself. Can I bust that all loose in just months? At all? I can't back off. I can't doubt. For brief moments I've considered ways to capitulate, to let it all fade away. And I am disgusted with myself for that.

He who hesitates is lost. I know that is absolutely true. But what do I do? I really think that I have just weeks, perhaps just days, to turn this around. Well, the best defense is a good offense. I'm a prosecutor; it's time to prosecute. By law, I am empowered to prosecute anyone, from the bottom to the top, but no one ever prosecutes the people at the top. It's professional suicide. That may well be, but I've got to do this.

But how do I do this? I can have subpoenas delivered to various Administrator's offices. I could, based on the available evidence in the leaks, have them physically arrested. That's all within my authority as the Prosecutor, but is it within my power? Can I make any of this happen, can I make it work, or will I be taken down and destroyed? There is no question that the Administrators will do anything they can to stem the tide. I need to find a way to have more power than them. It's a damn shame. John was right. Wanting to be free, and making yourself free are not the same thing. I just wanted to be free. Now, I have to fight for it. It occurs to me now; I might have to die for it. It's a sobering thought, but yes, here and now, I can say; I am willing to die for freedom.

I cannot hesitate. But I must not be a fool. I need allies. I know I have some, but who can I count on? So far, I think that I am still not suspected. I have to assume that I am not. I will get together with my compatriot and discuss this situation and form a strategy. If we can get reliable allies, we can hope to find a way to strike from within, before the Administrators realize we are not working for them, but against them.

I sat down with my compatriot. We spoke in 'code', as usual. "We have over a thousand people to prosecute, and the Administrators want them prosecuted immediately, and severely. The System isn't set up for this level or this type of prosecution. We need to structure a different program than what we currently have."

"There's no doubt about it," Ted responded. "It's well enough that the effort has been made to crack down on the subversive uprising taking place, but if we don't prosecute quickly and effectively, The System will look bad. It's in The System's best interest for us to be able move these cases quickly and with determination. But, how?"

"Well, I've been thinking. We need a special court, a court whose sole purpose is to handle cases brought to us in regard to these leaks. Anything related to them would go through this court. Since that would be its sole purpose, we could move cases through very effectively. The court should be exempted from the usual protocols intended to assure fair representation. That might be fine in normal times, but we need to be able to act more decisively in these times of extremism and civil unrest."

My compatriot took it from there. "Yes. We can't treat subversion like it's just some other minor offense. I've been very concerned about this entire chain of events. If we are to properly protect The System, which is what we are charged to do, we must have the authority to take whatever unique and specific actions that we deem necessary to protect it. We need a special court. And, I've been thinking also, for the sake of efficiency and effectiveness, it should have its own enforcement officers, so that there is no time lag or possible miscommunication between this new court and the Thought Police. The Thought Police are doing the best they can, and I respect them for that, but they would end up being a bottleneck in the court's operations. The court would need its own officers to serve subpoenas, make arrests, whatever."

"Good point," I said. "We must act fast, in order to bring things back under control."

We spent some hours honing details of the plan. We wrote up a proposal that we could present to our Division Head. If she went along, then it would go to the Central Planning Committee for approval. I would need to be able to pack this court with my own people. Packing agencies with allies and cohorts is normal, even expected. As long as no one suspected, I would get what I want. To start, I recommended Ted as the judge in this new "Subversion Abatement Court." Lorna didn't bat an eye at that. In fact, she was impressed with the plan. She may have glossed past the part where I would be an independent council, answerable to no one. Or maybe she noticed, and didn't see a problem.

Entry Forty-One

From two perspectives, time is of the essence. From my perspective, I need to develop enough power such that no one can stop me, and do it before I am discovered. For The System's part, they need to quickly get the leaks under control and get The People back into their submissive role.

So, the new court was authorized within forty-eight hours. Nothing happens that fast in The System. Until now. I have spent that time planning specific strategy, not least of all, who do I bring into my circle? For the sake of raw power, I need officers who will stick by me, no matter what. I have some good choices. My compatriot could name three who had contributed to the leaks file, and who had continued to be surreptitiously involved in the campaign. I brought them in. I knew two others myself, and brought them in. We've had to be cautious, so we didn't speak directly to what our intentions were but communicated all the same. And with all that has transpired recently, there is a multitude of people behind me. They are at various levels of authority, but they add up to quite a bit of power. I am hopeful.

That leaves Tracy. I have to think about her. If she is sympathetic to our cause, she could be highly effective. If not, well, she could still be highly effective, but in a bad way. If I play it safe, and leave her out, then sooner or later, probably sooner, she's going to see what's going on. And if it happened too soon, she could take me down. If I bought enough time, I might get set up solid before she could do anything. She is a conundrum.

In any event, it made sense to talk to her. I wanted everything she knew about the new Subversion Abatement Court to come from me. I called her into my office.

"Hello, Tracy. How's it going?"

"Pretty good. The other investigators and I are working away on all these subversion cases at the top."

"How are you doing? How are they doing?"

"Honestly, two of our investigators, I won't name names, seem kind of burnt out. I guess I understand, but we all have jobs to do."

She didn't need to name names; I knew she was talking about Carl and Andrew. But what were her observations? "So, are they burning out from the workload? Or don't they like what they're doing?"

"I don't think it's the workload. Rather, they seem a little too sympathetic to the suspects. I see their point, that way. Most of our defendants think of themselves as innocent people. They are so used to the way things work, they've never felt they were doing wrong. But they've done what they've done, and they have to be dealt with."

"And you know that's what this new court is about." I never told her that my compatriot and I created it. I wanted people to think it was created at the top, and that we were appointed, not virtually self-appointed. She wouldn't have to dig hard to find out that I created it, but would she? "Do you think it will improve the process?"

"No doubt about it."

"Did you know I've been named the special prosecutor to that court?" I watched her expression. It would tell me how much she already knew.

"Yes, it's been going around the office. Congratulations."

I still couldn't read her. "Given that I am, do you have any thoughts on the approach? You've always been on top of things, and I value your opinion."

"I'm looking forward to the cases moving through more quickly. The logjam isn't good for anyone. And if the court has more teeth, it will be easier to get suspects to turn over information. We can dig deeper quicker that way."

"Certainly. But I still want to plan an approach. Bottom up? Top down? Are there specific people or departments that should be targeted?"

She smiled. "I think you're supposed to tell me." I remained silent. She continued. "Like I said, when the subversives see we mean business, they'll be more inclined to implicate others. We started at the bottom, and we can work our way to the top. That's normal practice."

"Any department? Have you seen anything anywhere that's different from the others?"

"It's fairly random. I think CISA is cleaner, or at least it seems that way. I had the thought, though, that they might just be better at covering up."

"That's a concern, considering that they are the ones we're counting on to the find the sources of the signals." 'Signals' was a poor choice of words, and I immediately regretted saying it. It betrayed my knowledge that the posts were coming from an outside transmitter. She didn't seem to take any notice.

"I think about that, of course. I can't be sure. I've done the dance with Ken Stillers. You know, I question him, and he questions me. As with any suspect, you can't presume they're telling the truth."

"Is he a suspect?"

It was Tracy's turn to fall back. "Everyone is a suspect, is all. Until they're eliminated, everyone's a suspect."

"So, Ken, no more than anyone else? I need for you to be fully up front with me. You know what's at stake."

"Now you're treating *me* like a suspect!" she laughed.

"Not at all. But sometimes it's the little details that count."

"Of course. OK, frankly, there's something about Ken that doesn't click right. But it's one thing for someone to be a little less than forthcoming; it doesn't mean they're violating the law. I have nothing to indicate that he's not clean."

"Well, just keep me informed. Anyway, have you learned anything about their efforts to find the source of the origin of the leaks."

"They don't tell me everything, but they've told me that there seems to be some single source, but that the source is moving. That makes sense. If it was in one place all the time, I guess they'd find it quick enough."

"Yeah," I said. "I thought that all posts could be traced all the way back to their source. I'm surprised they can't find the source. Or block it, somehow."

"They can't block it; they've tried. It comes in on valid servers. They can't shut down all the servers. They even thought about that, but we could never shut down everything. The entire System would collapse."

"Sounds like they're getting nowhere," I offered.

"I think they're catching on. Even if they can't trace it, they're seeing some sort of patterns or something about the signals that help in tracing. They'll only tell me just so much, and I'm not that savvy anyway."

"Well, in the meantime it's on us to investigate. But that gets me to one last thing. I remember that you mentioned a while back that you were more concerned with corruption at the top than at the bottom. So am I. Would you be prepared to go straight to the top?

 "Yes! I've said that it's probably the top that is the real problem. It's getting them that's the tough part. You're the boss, point the way."

That's what I wanted to hear! Tracy seemed unbiased enough. She would go where the case took her. I just needed to help her with the direction.

Chip Kussmaul

Entry Forty-Two

The People are largely aware at this point that The System is corrupt. Some are deeply offended, feel betrayed, while others aren't really concerned. Within the system, there has been the routine show of concern over the leaks. The show consists of investigations, largely by my department, hearings, arrests, and trials. It makes for a good show, and satisfies many people. I think everyone knows it's largely a sham. For some, a sham, a good show, is all they want or need. But for others, they want honesty and integrity. I can only hope, and I do believe, that more and more people want the latter.

Until recently, I was just part of that show. We did the investigations, made the arrests, and prosecuted the trials. But it has all been curated. There has always been a layer of the bureaucracy above which we do not ascend. Now, we do. Having established the new Subversion Abatement Court, after becoming accepted by both The People and the Bureaucracy, it's time to make my move. Finally, I have more than just authority. I have power.

My court is well enough established, well enough accepted, even by The Bureaucracy (which should have known better), that I can move against them with at least a reasonable hope or prevailing. If I am wrong, and I don't pull this off, well, who knows? I've never had more reason to be afraid, and yet I have never felt so fearless.

Prior to now, lower-level offenders have been offered minimal plea deals. At the lower levels, the investigations and trials have begun and ended with convictions of these lower-level bureaucrats. Not anymore. I've instructed Tracy and the other investigators to make plea deals with defendants; rat out their superiors in exchange for leniency, even dismissal of charges. I had to contemplate, but I decided to make Tracy the lead negotiator, just as she has headed up all investigations. I think she can, and will, keep the others in line in the event of resistance.

I have no doubt that we can get to the top by doing this. Of course, the top will not sit still. They will come after me.

The People have already started to notice that the arrests and prosecutions for possessing subversive material have slowed to nearly nothing. I have seen to that. And that has emboldened them. Even more than before, the xerox fliers are everywhere. People are openly discussing matters that they could never discuss before. And what really counts, the defenders of The System can do no better than to make hollow arguments. Most everyone knows that the System is corrupt, even if not everyone will acknowledge it. Those who defend The System, who previously could gain some status from doing so, are now scoffed at. I don't know if long-held beliefs can be changed very quickly, if ever. But those who have put their trust in The System no longer enjoy acceptance and stature. *That* is what has changed.

And the Wall itself is seen in a new light. Instead of being seen as protection from outside forces, it is increasingly seen as a means of keeping us confined, both physically and spiritually. This may be the biggest thing of all. Nobody defends the Wall anymore. I mean, not in public sentiment. There are still the guards physically defending it, but there is no pretense. Defending the Wall is now more of a force of habit than part of anybody's conviction that it is needed to protect us.

Politics makes strange bedfellows, as they have said in the past. The head of the Wall Guard is dirty, like most of the Bureaucracy. We have more than enough to convict him. But instead, I made a deal. I said I would back off his investigation if he sent an order to The Guards to take no physical action against anyone who approached the Wall, even if they attempted to scale it or break it down. He is sworn

187

to claim it was his own initiative, and not directed by me. That will hold up just so long, but hopefully long enough for people to tear down the Wall.

And it's working. There have been ad hoc attacks on the wall. That is to say, some people have approached the wall to see if the Guards would really hold back. The Guards generally are very threatening, but as ordered, take no actual action. The Wall has been there as long as anyone remembers. I have to say, The Wall has been comforting, in people's minds. So, even free as they are to tear it down, there is not yet a groundswell to do it. But that time is coming!

Entry Forty-Three

For better or worse, I've noticed from reading my books that most revolutions don't happen with armies marching against each other. Yes, that happens. But most revolutions happen from the inside, politically. There used to be a term, 'banana republic'. It has little relationship to bananas, although the name relates to a time when the CIA set up friendly governments within tropical countries, many of which had bananas as their main crop. But you could as easily call them 'pineapple republics' or anything else. The point is, the CIA financed and engineered the overthrow of governments so that it could replace them with governments that it controlled. These were called 'coup d'état', the overthrow of the state. They invariably did it by secretly supporting and financing someone from within the targeted government. The CIA bought off the people it needed to buy, in order to get adequate support for these 'rebels'. They might actually win through a legitimate election. Or maybe they needed to rig the election. Worse case, supply the opposition with weapons and let them fight it out.

Even the American Revolution was somewhat like that. No CIA, of course; the revolution was long before the CIA. All the same, there were factions who favored continued rule by King George and there were those for revolution. The thing is, the leaders on *both* sides were all members of government. The Revolutionaries were not outsiders, they were already inside. Even after the revolution was officially over, and the United States of America became a reality, a constitutional republic, the very same people, the very same factions, continued on, struggling for political supremacy. The revolution changed things, but ended nothing.

I don't know whether any of this makes me feel better or worse. Does any of it justify or refute what I am doing? I am on the inside and, let's face it, I'm attempting a coup d'état. In all those other times, it seemed to me that the rebels, the revolutionaries, were the ones doing wrong. I still feel that way about the revolution in Russia under Lenin and the others. But I feel differently about the leaders of the American revolution under Washington and his compatriots. They did bring more freedom than there had been, but clearly not complete freedom. Can there be complete freedom?

I very much want to find some rationale that demonstrates that I am conclusively right. If it comes down to motives, then I am right. I want nothing for myself. I don't want power, but I must have it to achieve worthwhile ends. Am I rationalizing, or am I indisputably in the right? They say that the victor writes the history books. True enough. I've never seen a book from King Geroge's point of view. Russia, ultimately the Soviet Union, has rewritten its own history multiple times. When Lenin was in control, and then Stalin, the Russian history books praised their successes and ignored the tens of millions who died under their rule. Later, though, the statues of Lenin came down. Yet Stalin became even more revered, decades after his death. They were both mass murderers. Don't just study the history, study the historians.

There was the novel, 1984, which made an eerie assessment of the time in which it was written, 1948. It pretended to represent the future, but really, it was about the present. Why do we need fiction to tell us the truth? When the truth is right there to be seen, why do we need to discover it in a work of fiction?

Entry Forty-Four

It's coming down to the wire! I'm tense, but resolved. Succeed, or die trying. Tracy and her team have done a great job of turning low level perpetrators into unidentified whistleblowers. We are roaming around within the very top ranks. Two department heads have given up. They have resigned, one 'for health reasons' and the other to 'have more time with family'. The Department of Education and the CDC now have temporary heads. They will need permanent heads, and I find myself with more influence than I realized. Nobody in The System wants to be in my crosshairs. Some come to me, currying my favor, seeking my approval of matters that should not involve me. Thus, I am being consulted in advance about who the new permanent department heads should be. I make my own recommendations, if only in an unofficial capacity. The interesting thing is, I have no authority to have that influence, but I have that power.

The Wall doesn't even matter anymore. It is being torn down in whatever areas people feel like going to the trouble. Some people were panicked that all hell would break loose if The Wall was breached, but there have been no real problems. My people have the momentum. The System is physically and spiritually in retreat. Its leaders used to fiercely defend it, now they just try to cover their own butts.

But then, I got a call from Sarah. As soon as I saw her name on the screen, my heart sank.

"Hello, Sarah. How are you doing? Is everything all right?"

"I'm fine. But I know you've been concerned about my mother's cancer, and you wanted to be kept up to date."

191

Chip Kussmaul

My heart was pounding. It almost didn't matter anymore, what Sarah had to say concerning any CISA intelligence. I already had so much under control. But still… "Of course, I very much care about her. Your mother means a lot to me."

"Well, the doctors have found something they hadn't been able to see before. I don't know the specifics of such things, but they tell me that they have some new scanning technique that allows them to see things they couldn't see before. Honestly, it doesn't look good for my mother. Of course, I'd rather know about this than not. It's just that I felt so much better before."

"I know exactly what you mean. So, when did they do this new scan? When did they determine the new issues?"

"Not long ago, I don't think. I think this is it, the end"

"Well, I'm so sorry to hear about that, but I guess it was to be expected, sooner or later. I hate to cut you off like this, but I've had something come up that I have to deal with immediately."

"Of course. I know you're busy."

We hung up, and I pulled the little walkie-talkie out of my pocket. I pressed the transmit button. "Shut it all down, NOW!" I said to whoever it was that was listening.

I've felt anonymous, sitting here at this antique laptop, for these several years. Doing this is better than a Counselor Nanny, by far. Counselor Nannies shape you into the expectations of others. This laptop and I have shaped me into who I am. I was so uncertain at first, afraid of being found out. This laptop, if discovered, could have been my ruin. Now, I have no reason for concern. So much has changed! I am more sure of who I am, and I insist on the right to be who I am. The System is, well, let's just say it is less sure of itself.

I was afraid of this diary being discovered, now I am contemplating releasing it to The People. It may become a manifesto of sorts. Not a manifesto declaring that all should be like me, but that all should seek their own selves.

Freedom is a lot of damned work. Risky, even. In my dreams, everyone craves to do that work, take those risks. But I know it's not true. I am free. Yet I can't leave here. I spent all this effort, am taking all these risks, such that I would be able to walk out the gate in the Wall, turn around and say goodbye on my own terms. But I can't leave. Too much depends on me. Have I trapped myself? Is my prison of my own making? I remember a song by Kris Kristofferson, some sort of folk singer. There is a line in one of his songs, "Freedom's just another word for nothing left to lose." I think of that line continually, these days.

Chip Kussmaul

Entry Forty-Five

Some revolutions take years. Some are overnight. Some succeed. Some fail. Out of all of those possibilities, the one that I can cross off the list for this revolution is 'overnight.' It's been nearly a year since my compatriot and I finagled our own court, under the guise of defending The System. It's working, for the most part. It comes down to how many friends I have, and who will stand with me. Times like this tell you who your friends really are.

CISA, specifically Ken Stillers, had caught on to our communications system a little ahead of when Sarah found out and told me. Fortunately, John had been so mobile that Stillers found little of what he hoped to find. Raids yielded no one. But he had become aware of some key locations, and there were old security videos that he could bring up. He had video of me going into the law office to see John, where other operatives, 'subversives', had been known to go. With me as a suspect, he could pinpoint times and places where I had met with John's people. He had listened in on Sarah's warning to me. He checked, and there was no news for her to report concerning her mother. The good news is that his case is mostly circumstantial. Nothing he has on record directly implicates me, but when you connect the dots, a person would have to know that I am at the center of the leaks.

So, I wasn't surprised when Tracy came into my office and asked to talk. I invited her in, and she closed the door behind her and took one of the chairs in front of my desk.

We regarded each other, but neither of us spoke. We both knew that a good professional relationship was about to end, probably in turmoil. Neither of us wanted to move past the silence, but it couldn't stay this way. I offered her an opening.

"Have you talked to Ken Stillers lately?"

Even with the prompt, she was hesitant. "Yes," she said, finally. "Quite a bit." She paused again, to form her words. "I've been reconstructing the last year or so, based on what he's had to tell me." She waited for me to respond, but I didn't. "And we've tracked the leaks through the process of elimination… They all lead back to you."

I was glad that there was not accusation in her voice, so much as resignation. I had let her down. She had trusted me, and I let her down. She had done the job she was appointed to do, was directed by me to do, and now here we were. Funny, I felt no guilt over all my actions, all that I had done. I felt guilty only about having manipulated Tracy. The rest could be equivocated, but not that.

"I'm sorry I ever put you in this position," I said. "You are one of the most honest, reliable people I know, and you are owed the utmost consideration and respect." What more could I say? "Out of all that's gone on here the last two years, my one real regret is this, this meeting with you right now. But, can I be honest?"

"That would be nice."

"I have no other regrets. I've been a lawyer too long to state specifics here, but we know what we're talking about. Dare I say, I think we're still on the same side? We prosecute criminals and criminal offences. It's what we're supposed to be doing. It's what we've been doing, and I'm glad. I think I've been a benefit."

Tracy studied me silently. Whatever she decided, might determine my future. "Ken wanted me to go undercover to get you. He wanted to interview me to come up with enough to prosecute you. I declined. Of course, his office can't prosecute, so it comes back to our office.

And it comes back, pretty much, to your court and me." She paused as we both contemplated what we knew she would say next. "What I do from here, is likely to be the deciding factor. If I go with Ken, he can probably take you down, with my help. If I don't, you can probably take him down. With my help." She saw me silently confirm her thought. "What do you think I should do?"

It was an interrogator's question. What I wanted her to do was obvious enough. How I answered would make the difference. To my credit, I have never been good at vapid bullshit. If I had tried it, she would have gone straight to Ken. "I'd do it all again. Frankly, I don't intend to stop. Where it goes from here, I don't know. We don't know. But I won't stop. But you can trust me on this; I will never turn against your integrity. Whatever you decide, I will accept your actions. That's not to say I will ever capitulate, but you won't have to watch your back."

"To what end do you intend to keep doing this? Was it really so bad before? Is it really better now?"

"Yes, it was really that bad before. People get used to things. People get cancer, and in the end, they may have to just get used to it, and even get used to knowing they will die too soon. But, given a choice, you excise the cancer. I was used to the life we had. I could live with it, make a nice living from it. But I find I'd rather be free. It's work. Freedom is a lot more damned work than just going along. But it's worth it." I wasn't making a case, the way a good lawyer does. I was not calculating and figuring what Tracy would respond to. I was just being honest. Let the chips fall as they may. Given how honest she is, that's probably for the best anyway.

She continued to study me. Strangely, I felt comfortable. Honesty is such a comfortable feeling. Then, she said, "I'm going to have to think about his, if only for a short while. I know this situation isn't going to sit and wait for me. In fact, Ken made an ultimatum. Report to him by the end of the day, or he's coming after me as well as you."

I nodded. "Well, I want you to consider this: If you stay with me and I lose, you are in big trouble. If you go with Ken and I win, you are not. You would only have to be honest, and there will never be repercussions from me. Ken does what he does because it is his nature to scheme and build coalitions and amass power. I do what I do in the hope that we can all have our own lives and be free from all of that." There was nothing more for me to say.

Tracy smiled wanly. I smiled back. She rose, and I rose with her. For the first time in a long time, we shook hands as she was leaving. "No matter what," she said, "I'll talk to you before I talk to Ken." She opened the door and left.

Chip Kussmaul

Entry Forty-Six

Tracy stayed with me. Ken has agitated, in any way he can think of, to get me and my people thrown off the court. But he doesn't have the allies that I do, and, so far, he is losing. I haven't arrested him at this point, because he also has allies, and I have to step lightly, and carefully. The People, who can now freely exchange information and ideas, are largely behind me. I now see how important free speech is, over and above our rights to it. Ken, for his part, is trying to restrict speech, and I think that is working against him, not for him.

I get to see Sarah without pretense. She is what they used to call a 'hot potato'. Or better yet, a well-placed pawn. She cannot attack, but neither can she be attacked, because of her position. Even though Ken knows what she contributes to my power base, he keeps her on in his office. He knows well the old saying, 'Keep your friends close; keep your enemies closer'. Even at CISA, there are those who are behind Sarah, at least in sentiment. Ken cannot make a move against her that would not play against his efforts to project impartiality. And I am here to prosecute him if he should attempt it.

Guilt, Innocence. Interesting concepts that they teach in law school. Politics knows none of that. In politics it's coalitions, publicity, manipulation, and power plays. I have learned to play the game. It's an ugly, offensive game that I don't want to have to play, that I don't even want to watch from the sidelines. But there are no sidelines in a free society. We're in it, all the time. Or else.

Chip Kussmaul

Acknowledgements:

To my wife, Jan, who knows me better than anyone, and loves me anyway.

Thanks to various readers who have done much to make this work better—Jan, Barb, Betty, Randi, Don, Tom, Carol, and my cohorts at the Cincinnati Writer's Project.

ABOUT THE AUTHOR:

Chip Kussmaul is a retired public school teacher and businessman. Most of his professional life centered around engineering and fabrication. Now, in retirement, he is finally getting to put his English degree to good use. When he is not writing under his real name, he writes under his pseudonym, The Radical Individualist. Much of his work can be found at his Substack site, IndividualistsUnite.Substack.com

IndividualistsUnite.com

IndividualistsUnite.Substack.com

Chip Kussmaul

www.ingramcontent.com/pod-product-compliance
Lightning Source LLC
Chambersburg PA
CBHW060318310726
48976CB00007B/2377